BEYOND
GLASS

Beyond Glass

by

Rachel Knightley

Black Shuck Books
www.BlackShuckBooks.co.uk

Versions of the following stories first appeared as follows:
'Wolf in the Mirror' in *Writers Forum Magazine* (2016)
'Green Lady' in *Legacies of Loss* (University of Hull, 2019)

Cover design & internal layout © WHITEspace 2021
www.white-space.uk

978-1-913038-99-1

In memory of Jim Craddock
and Dr Charlie Allbright

When we suffer, we have a choice to be crushed or transformed.
We either mourn and grow or switch off and curse the world.

Malcolm Stern
interview with Psychologies Magazine
December 2020

They tried to bury us.
They did not know we were seeds.

Mexican proverb

The Other
Woman,
Part 1

'You knew,' Holly says.

Summer beats lightly on the garden room's glass ceiling above us. At the bottom of the garden, somewhere beyond the willow trees, the barbecue is starting its first quiet crackles. The sunlight and Holly's stare, which is warmer than the sun, prickle the side of my cheek. If I try very hard, I won't feel anything beyond all this.

'Joy?'

'What?' I watch the willows, their calm and predictable pendulum-sway. The tiniest of breezes fills the perfectly ordered room with the promise of spring. It feels like a promise meant for someone else.

'You knew. Long before there was any blood.'

'Did I?' I turn from the middle distance to the opposite sofa, as guarded as it's possible to be against this other version of my own face. 'Knew what?'

'I just mean...' Holly props herself higher on the cushions, her manicured toes gripping the edge of the glass coffee table. That table was a gift from me, one I never thought to get for myself, even when I finally got my own place. Things always look better on Holly. Holly is why I can't blame my cheekbones for my skeletal face. Holly is the reason I know that never knowing what to do with my hair is all about me, not about it. Holly is how I know I'm not as short as I choose to walk; that I've somehow chosen to be "the short twin" even though we're exactly the same height.

And another thing about Holly: she radiates time. For health, for sleep. For taking nail polish off before it chips. For getting things done, work finished, bills paid.

For breaking up with people before someone dies.

I scratch at the edges of the last of the French manicure Nick liked so much. Holly would have called the police, the first time Virginie turned up. Holly wouldn't have been so desperate to see the thing through, wouldn't have invested so hard in Nick's sense of empowerment in dealing with it himself. Holly wouldn't have needed to know how the story ended, and let herself become its victim. Holly would not have ended up dismantling her life, under police escort, and squatting in her twin's attic.

'I just mean I'm glad you're here,' Holly says.

And not dead: the affix hangs in the afternoon air. I kick one battered trainer against the other. Nothing hurts. The life I've dismantled is unreal, distant and separate as the sun on Holly and Tom's glass roof. The proximity in time (a week? Two? Days went on repeat the moment the police disconnected my mobile) and space (less than a mile) is unreal, wrong. How could Tom and Holly's house be in the same universe, let alone the same postcode, as all that blood?

'I'm not saying you're wrong,' I tell her. 'I'm just saying a hug and a box of Maltesers would be better than being right.'

She looks at me for a moment, and I spot genuine worry. Strange. Holly only worries about things she can change. Then she changes them. Then she stops worrying. I've never seen anything fall between those categories. 'You did though,' she says.

'Did what?'

'You knew. Saw the...' Here it comes. It was Dad's favourite saying. Holly took it up before she knew what the words meant and has never put it down. 'The Opportunity In The Crisis. You saw it.'

'No, just the blood.' But even that's not true. Mainly what I see now are all the moments before. Mainly I see Nick parking his motorbike with shaking, careful hands in my drive – "I've done it!" – his face ablaze with such pride, such delight, green eyes wide and bright as a child winning their first medal at sports day, the door to a new world they've opened up by their own ability, their own free will. "I've left Virginie!"

In that moment, I only saw his eyes. But then he lifted off his helmet and I registered the purple oval lump eclipsing his right temple, the letterbox-slit of scarlet that bisected it. That was the first blood, though at the time I took it for the last. Why wouldn't I? How could blood not signal the end?

It didn't occur to me that you could see your own blood and still choose to go back. It never occurred to me what would occur to anyone who'd read the statistics I've been googling from then until the police took my phone and email offline: how many domestic violence victims go back, and go back and go back.

I didn't see a statistic. I saw Nick. So there I sat, on the edge of the bath in the flat I'd bought believing it would be ours, cleaning his headwound and allowing him to talk me out of calling the police because "what I had to understand about Virginie was...". I don't remember what. I didn't care. He was here, now. He was safe. He'd made his choice to move on, evolve, build a real love, make a choice based on who he was and not a debt to who he once had been. I could be magnanimous, not call the police. Because I believed that was what was happening, that it had already happened. I didn't say anything when he slept with a can of cider by the bed. I didn't say anything when it was two. Of course he'd need time to recover. Of course I could bend my own rules, ignore my own instincts. Of course I could. Every one of them. And of course it only got easier to keep on bending.

'Name one,' says Holly. 'One situation. Where it doesn't apply. The Opportunity In Every Crisis.'

'Cystitis.' I glare through my glasses into what are, to all intents and purposes, my own eyes, though her contacts make them a clearer blue than my smeared lenses. 'Thrush. Cancer.'

'Wrong. You're wrong.' She almost sings it, in a tone others might reserve for "happy birthday". 'I got cystitis once.' She's so proud you'd think she was talking about the George Cross. 'It made me get back in touch with Anisha. Remember Anisha? The old schoolfriend I missed so much and never knew why we lost touch? I remembered she was a GP, and mine were being useless, so I messaged her. On Twitter.'

Another barb. My refusal to engage in social media, Holly's ultimate proof I'm irredeemable. The last thing I want is a thousand voices shouting at me every moment, when the one soft, high-pitched voice that's still as clear in my head in as it was in my ear in the days when I was allowed to answer my own phone, that still makes me shake whenever I see "unknown caller", is there all the time.

'Anisha lives in Mortlake, would you believe? Practically next door. Tom and I often run into her now, never would have recognised her if we hadn't got in touch. Must have walked past each other any number of times...'

She's waiting to say what she really wants to say, wearing through the conversation in layers, anaesthetising before she gets to the bone. I don't try to help. There is no rush, nothing to hurry from or to.

'There's nothing wrong with needing people, Joy. Needing people is an opportunity. To connect. To be part of a community. Actually,' she pushes a perfectly tidy strand of hair behind her ear. 'I wanted to tell you about that. You might want to get involved. It is a community, really. A work hub. Everybody helps each other with whatever comes up...'

'Sure,' I say. 'Maybe.' It's like staring at two separate worlds, my scratched, worn trainers on their thick carpet. There's so much space at Tom and Holly's, as well as so much time. My home (when it was my home) is (was) hurried. You could tell from everywhere that time moved too fast. Objects plonked where they probably ought to be, or where I happened to be. Things left out because they might be needed. All packed too close together as if all on permanent alert, expecting to be deployed at any minute.

Everything that makes Holly and Tom's place their own has settled into position as if it belongs there and always has; clean and confident and restful as fallen snow. 'I didn't know I was a mistress until I knew I had a stalker,' I say.

Holly pushes a long, tidy curl behind her ear, and waits.

'I knew Nick lived with the mother of his adult son. I knew he and the mother had separate bedrooms. I knew her name was Virginie. That they were from the same part of Paris but met in London. That she was fifteen years older than him. All his friends knew all of that. I knew Paul, their son, had never known it any other way.' Holly makes a noise of acceptance, not sympathetic enough to derail me, just enough to let me know she's there in the silence. Space and time hang in the air, stretch around this circle of transparent grey glass under Holly's feet, touch the perfectly stacked bookshelves, the spirits and mixers in the central shelf, the mirror above the drinks cabinet reflecting perfect order back at itself. In the mirror is the reverse of Van Gogh's *Starry Night*, framed in mahogany, with the frizzy brown suggestion of my own head the smallest of interruptions beneath. A jasmine candle burns on the mantelpiece, but I've sat here too long to be able to smell it. 'In my ten years of friendship with Nick, there were at least three others. Proper girlfriends. You met them, didn't you?'

Holly nods. 'At different parties, sure.'

'You see? You barely knew him and *you* knew.'

'You just didn't think to ask, did Virginie know?'

Her name on Holly's lips sends a jolt of cold over my skin, a slap in the face that somehow covers every cell in my body. Worse than hearing it from the police, or in my own mind, is hearing it on the lips of my family. That this can touch them. It makes that high-pitched, girlish voice all too real, all too present again. The sort of voice you'd think couldn't lift a knife, let alone use it. 'No.'

'No?'

'No, Holly, I didn't see the opportunity. I didn't even see the crisis.' I sigh, stare harder into the carpet. 'The first night Virginie found my address and turned up at our front door, I knew it was her from the doorbell. We were on the sofa, watching *Ever After*. I was calling the title a spoiler; Nick said it couldn't be because it didn't have the word "happy" first. "Ever after" could mean anything. Hell as likely as heaven. Then the bell rang.' I try to keep breathing around the pictures as they return, the home that stopped being mine when she stood outside it. 'An identical ring to every time it had rung before, yet something still told me...'

Holly waits.

'Nick looked at me, I looked at him, reading the fear in his eyes but not realising till later it was just a reflection of my own. I peered through the letterbox; there was... just this rectangle of woman. This vivid cerise sweater, a little too tight, chewed emerald fingernails gripping a brown leather handbag strap so hard the fingertips were turning white. I remember I said, "Who is it?" And I almost felt like laughing, the question so stupid especially when I knew the answer. But those were the only words that fitted the gap, put a block before what would happen next began. "Nick's sweetheart," she said. That strange trilling little voice, Holly. She sounded so *innocent*. I knew. I hadn't heard her voice before but...'

'It fitted.'

'Yes.' I look at Holly. 'He didn't understand why I wouldn't invite her in. He just didn't associate the lump still healing on his temple with the woman standing outside our front door. He wasn't even surprised she had the address. Why would you do that, why would you give your address to someone who'd put you in so much danger?'

Holly swallows whatever answer she wants to give. Instead, she says 'What did you do?'

'Waited. Turned the lights off. They stood outside and talked while I sat in the dark and listened. I suppose I thought – if I thought at all – I was empowering him. Giving him the chance to finally, decisively show her he chose this. Letting him hear himself tell her. Maybe that's what I thought the opportunity in the crisis was. That if this was what he needed, to hear himself telling her it's over, this was it. The opportunity.'

'And?'

'And she said... I heard her say...' I don't want to say this bit. Not to Holly. This bit will be worse than the far worse bits that follow. 'She called me what she knew took our mother.'

'She called you a cancer.' Holly's voice is colder now.

I nod, my eyes following the fibres of Holly's thick, safe carpet. '"This girl is a cancer, she is a cancer eating you." She used all the others too: "homewrecker", "slut", "gyppo"...'

'Wait. What?'

'That was another thing he said I "had to understand about Virginie". It was different in Paris, he said.'

Holly's eyebrows climb her forehead. 'Virginie is not Paris's fault. If he thinks it is, then she's not the only racist.'

'In the end he walked her back to the station, not telling me where he was going, not saying goodbye. Later he told me they'd "gone to a café for a nice chat". I asked him if he didn't think she'd attack him again. He laughed, like that was the oddest idea in the world. He said no, she only lashed out when she was upset...'

I don't trust my voice to get more information out. I can see every millimetre of the bruises on his arms, the crack of blood on his forehead that hadn't healed then, hadn't even healed in the photos the police eventually let me see when I convinced them how much worse it would be not to see, not to know.

'I wanted to rescue him. I wanted to give him the chance to rescue himself.'

'You weren't wrong to try,' Holly says.

'Thank you.' She doesn't mean it. She can't. How could she when, now I say all this, it sounds so foolish I can't imagine anyone else believing it, let alone that I did. Because why, after all, shouldn't Nick give her my address and invite danger, when I'd kept on doing the same in giving it to him? Why should I believe he'd broken his addiction to a person who came with danger when I hadn't broken mine?

'Maybe it saved you. Being stupid this time. Maybe that's the opportunity.'

'Yeah. Thanks a lot.'

'Seriously. Knowing how you got yourself into this means you'll know when another disaster comes towards you, before it happens. Like getting lost in broad daylight somewhere, the next time you're there might be dark and you'll not get lost then, because you found the way before. How's the coffee?'

'It's perfect,' I say, more as accusation than compliment.

'You haven't drunk it.'

'I know how we make coffee.'

She returns the smile I thought I'd hidden. The recognition that *we* is really *he*. Dad taught us to make coffee so strong Mum used to call it marmite. 'So. Look...' Holly opens the tin that sits on the incomprehensibly tidy table. 'I was telling you about the work community? This exchange-of-favours work we do? Raking leaves, going to the post office, doing accounts...'

'Sure. Great. Maybe.' Outside the window, a wasp flies right towards us, bounces and ricochets off the glass before flying out of sight.

'It's great, Joy. You take on whatever task someone else is too emotionally involved to deal with. House clearance, pest control, changing gas supplier... whatever stresses you out, whatever you're overthinking, someone else just gets it done. If you read the list, everything on it sounds tiny. Except for the thing you put on yourself, which of course sounds huge...'

A crumb from my biscuit drops into my coffee. The black circular tides spread outward, rippling towards the rim, before they reach their confines and disappear. Holly's mugs have the huge surface area we weren't allowed at home.

The one thing our parents agreed on, which Dad got harder on us with when it was just him, was there was no point in a wide surface area, because the drink cools off too fast, so you have to drink it fast to enjoy it ("That's life," I remember shouting at Dad. Or did I mumble it? And was it me, or was it Holly?). 'And there's one you want me to do?'

'Then when someone in the community accepts the job, whoever needs the favour done gets to walk away, go to a café or whatever, and when they walk back into their life the problem's gone away. Solved. It might be good for you.' Holly sips from the edge of her mug. 'Get your confidence back. And you can put something else you need on the list. Then someone, me or one of the others, sorts out your problem for you.'

'Why do I feel I'm joining a cult?'

She laughs, for just a little too long. 'Is that a yes? Because it will be great. All the mental admin that stopped you calling the police earlier, standing in your own way, asking yourself what kind of person it made you instead of what needs to be done...'

'Okay, I get the idea.'

'Like when Nick talked you out of calling the police. And you did what he wanted instead of what you knew would have worked. The people on this list actually *want* to lay their ghosts to rest. You thought his motive was to break the circle, get out of limbo. You didn't accept he'd been perfectly content there for years because you were too close. Take Nick arriving at your door, bleeding from the head, saying he'd left her having sworn to you they weren't together in the first place and hadn't been for years.'

I hadn't thought of it that way. 'What about it, Holly?'

'Goodies and baddies. That's your problem. Once you knew she was a violent racist bully, saving him was a red rag to a bull. Nothing would have stopped you. You saw the dragon's mouth and charged right in.'

'I what?' But I get it, the dragon reference, the handsome prince I thought I was saving. I can't even defend myself with my favourite argument, that had mine and Nick's genders been reversed everyone would see the whole thing differently, that a woman returning to a man with a history of violence would have been a totally different conversation. I'd still tried to do the leaving for him, and that was never going to work.

'Just...' Holly hides in a sip of coffee, a fierce and vulnerable look sheltering itself in her view of the distance beyond the window. 'Maybe next time you'll wait, see what they do, not what they say. See if they're on their own side. If they want to be rescued.'

'But what if they don't?'

'Then they don't,' says Holly. 'Want it. The help. Which means it isn't help.'

'Maybe.' Every night in the dark beside me I can still hear the sound of his fingernails sliding up and down the pillow, a loud and continuous scratch that told me, if I'd only listened, that he wasn't really here, had escaped but hadn't left. And with every explanation – "Virginie was angry, so she threw my iPad at my head", "What you have to understand about Virginie is she gets angry so she has to hit me" – all I did was try harder to give the help I wanted him to want.

He went back "for a night or two" within a week, saying that was the best way to let her come to terms with him leaving. When he returned when he said he would, I thought it was a good sign. Then he said, chatting over the washing up, "I told her all about you."

"What did you say?" I asked. I remember putting a plate down, as if I already knew what the answer was able to do to me. The sun was streaming through the kitchen window, him washing the plates and me drying. If anyone had walked past that day (the day the blinds went up for the first time since she'd found my address), what they'd see would look perfectly normal.

Nick looked up into my eyes with that same pride and enthusiasm with which he'd told me he'd left her and said, "I wanted her to like you. To understand why I love you so much."

I waited.

"I told her you're a poet and you teach poetry. Remember I told you she always wanted to be a teacher? Always loved poems? And I told her you're third-generation Romanian." I felt my throat tighten. It was only when we were together he said, as if talking about a fear of spiders or a dislike of a particular shade of pink, *You have to understand about Virginie, she's got this... thing about immigrants...* And then he told me why it was understandable because everyone in her family hated immigrants. I knew that he was a person

- 28 -

who didn't see racial hatred of me as a reason not to be with someone. And that I was a person who would be with that person. And that was when I knew that in loving him I didn't know who I was. "And that you're fifteen years younger than me." He smiled, as if we were in on the same joke. "The same amount she's older than me."

"Are you doing this on purpose?" It was the only time I ever asked him.

Even as he looked up at me like he didn't understand the question, I didn't turn it in, ask it of myself.

"You've told your violent racist ex that your Roma girlfriend is everything she ever wanted to be...*so she'd like me?*"

And there were those big innocent eyes again.

'Joy? What are you thinking about?'

'Nothing.' What else was there to think about? What would there ever be?

'What happened next?'

'When I got tired of the missed calls and blocked her mobile, then blocked their son's mobile, the emails started. I was a filthy gyppo who didn't understand love, I was a homewrecking slut and I was going straight to hell. That following me to work down Regent Street she'd seen the proof that devils walk the Earth. That I was destroying their child's happiness, that he would never recover from his father's betrayal.'

'Yet Nick said they weren't together for...?'

'All their son's life! He'd said it before we were together! We were friends! I didn't have any reason not to believe him!'

'You tried to help,' says Holly. 'The opportunity was getting away with your life.'

I nod. 'When Nick mentioned she regularly read his email so I might want to try only texting him, I showed him how to change his password. When she found she couldn't open his email, she called him immediately, screaming "Your devil slut is stealing your inbox for herself". Her little voice, it filled our kitchen. The phone right to his ear, as if the sound didn't hurt him, he looked at me like he'd never seen me before. He believed her interpretation of the facts he'd witnessed and she hadn't.'

'Did you see her again?'

'Only once. She followed us down the street, tapped him on the shoulder. He was holding my hand. Everything was so wonderfully normal. I didn't know how perfect it was until she appeared. Asked me if I knew he'd lived with her, that they had a child... What could I say? Your child is twenty-five and you're a physically violent racist? How would that have helped? He walked her back to the station, they had another coffee. Then he came home and made me feel foolish for wanting to call the police. Yet in her racism, her violence, her staying together in the name of the child rather than living separate, happy, real lives – each of us saw pure evil. Don't you think that's interesting?'

Holly's toes curl on the edge of the table. 'Interesting?'

'That the person who represents pure evil to me, believes that's exactly what I am too?'

'*Interesting?*'

'I mean...' My nails are sharp in my clenched hands, willing her to agree, to see Virginie's point of view as Nick was desperate for me to. 'Worth thinking about?'

'Evil isn't subjective, Joy! Good and evil aren't like having a different favourite fucking colour to someone else!'

'But you said I was wrong to believe in goodies and baddies.'

'Evil is an objective fucking reality.' Holly's anger is not the usual, habitual disappointment about how much more I could let myself have, let myself be. This time she's angry *for* me. 'It's the worst of us, the worst and the cruellest. Fear made flesh. How can you not see what no amount of his own blood ever told him?'

'I...' My eyes gravitate to the safety of the willows.

'Because if you've learnt nothing, then he's dead for nothing.'

He'd gone back to get his passport when it happened. Virginie was five foot four with a small, soft voice: none of the neighbours stepped in to protect him from himself in going back, even when they heard the same old screams. There was nothing new in it, they didn't hear any difference through the walls when she grabbed the knife.

But blaming other people's limited imaginations doesn't change my own. If Virginie was a perpetrator, then Nick was a victim. He could tolerate having his mobile phone thrown at his head by a woman because she claimed to love him. He could not tolerate being rescued by one.

And he went back, to talk to her, video-called me from the living room, turned to me with those same big blue eyes and said "She's left a note, saying she's going back to Paris tomorrow, she understands we're both moving on. She's letting us be together!"

Suddenly, and finally, I knew what anyone who didn't care too much would have assumed. That twenty-five years meant he wasn't staying for the sake of his son; that him standing on video-call in their empty flat and looking at me with that same shining face, believing he could only do what Virginie let him and that she was about to change, showed he wasn't safe, and never would be, and neither would I: that my addiction to him was no different to his addiction to her.

Maybe I'll always be asking myself what I really thought, what I would have done; whether I'd come good on the realisation and stepped away. But by then the chance to ever know was gone, because then I saw his eyes move, shift left in a tiny jolt, but changing his whole face in the process, as if at some level he already knew everything that was about to happen as he heard Virginie's key in the lock. When I close my eyes,

I still see and still try to read the dozens of expressions that seemed to pass over his face in the two seconds before he said "I'll call you back." Then his voice and picture disappeared.

I didn't worry for the first twelve hours or so. He'd often gone off radar for days at a stretch, having "one last day out" with Virginie, "one last dinner". There'd even been "one last holiday" I'd discovered from a ticket stub that even now I was too ashamed to tell Joy I'd found and still not given up on him.

But it wasn't Nick who finally came to the door.

The police told me it was neighbours of Nick and Virginie's who'd called them in, one of the neighbours who identified Nick's body. They'd often ignored the screams, but they couldn't ignore the smell. They'd known these arguments, years of them, but the horror had not occurred to their imaginations, was no more real than a movie, because it was a woman they heard yelling at a man. A woman they knew to be below average height, with greying hair. A tiny woman with a tiny voice, trying to bellow in her high-pitched squeak at her biker husband. This marriage was comedy, not tragedy.

"But they never married," I told the police, as I'd told my friends, on repeat, as if it changed a thing: his choices, or his death. "They never married. He wasn't her..." He wasn't hers. No one is someone else's to keep. But he let himself believe he was, because he didn't know how to be his own.

'Why would you hit and hit and hit?'

Holly shrugs. 'Because it worked and it worked and it worked?'

I look out of Holly's front window, let my eyes defocus over the leafy series of backstreet gardens lying silently beside each other. Holly and Tom's sash window and net curtains perfectly mirror the sash window and net curtains of the house opposite. You don't have to be a twin to wonder how much is true identity and how much is reflection, how much is who we are and how much a repeat performance of whatever we see. Nick was exactly my age now when he lost his virginity to Virginie, in her attic bedroom. I picture a bohemian haven, stars outside, a thin window. Then I try and imagine twenty-five years of the person you think definitive reinforcing the idea, making themselves and not you the centre of your world.

I look at my twin, the most real person in my world. What if the most present, solid and dependable person had been a lover, instead of a sister? Someone whose morality included physical violence and race hate, but who considered my religion or culture made me evil? I wonder who he would have been, if he hadn't found her to reflect.

'Remember when you chose the colours for this room?' Holly asks.

I look up again. 'Yes.' It could be someone else's memory. I can't remember who I was when it happened. Odd to think I was instrumental in creating this place, that I'd chosen the colour scheme I've been comparing myself unfavourably with ever since. 'I'd forgotten that.'

'It was only a month or two before you and him.' She lets that drop into the silence, like the biscuit crumb into the coffee, lets the ripples subside before she goes on. 'Even your voice changed. You became so... incomplete, uncertain. It's like you built a tower to lock yourself in, just to try and get him to rescue you.'

'And neither of us rescued each other.'

She shrugs. 'You gave him everything he

needed to save himself.' She shakes her head, almost too slight to see. 'I can't believe they let you see the pictures.'

'They let me see because I asked to see.' Nick looked so recognisable, so very much himself, that it was almost a relief, seeing him in the crime scene photos after all that silence. It surprised me that so much blood could flow so widely from such a small space. Particularly when he'd fallen face down, the knife below the centre of his back. After all those threats, she only had to mean it once. She'd moved him afterwards, her bloodied handprint on his cheek, the side of his shirt, before she left. A day isn't so long if you know it's ending, but the gaps were always infinite, always with the idea wobbling on the edge of my mind that my worst fears about Virginie – the ones he'd thought so funny, so far from the truth of how he saw their arguments – would come true.

Now here it was, the end of the story. All his stories – the throwing things at each other, the strangling each other on Richmond Hill – I always knew one of those stories might not end in him telling me about it. I try to imagine what the son they'd stayed together for would take away from that, and shiver. Wherever she was now, they'd find her. But what was clear, the inspector added, was Nick had been turning away, leaving the kitchen, on the way to the front door. In the very end, Nick had meant to leave her.

'What are you thinking?'

I'm thinking about the unmarked police car parked permanently outside Tom and Holly's house. I'm thinking about the strangers' cars and mirroring net curtains in every window of every house the length of the street. I'm thinking how every façade can hide its own crime scene, or its crime-scene-to-be. How any of those identical pictures could have another Virginie looking back right now. Above all, what growing up with that kind of normalcy – when good was frightening people out of leaving, and evil was being from another country and religion – has done to the man Paul has become. 'I'm thinking Virginie's going to find me before they find her.'

'Virginie will be found,' says Holly, and this time her voice is all fire. 'I promise you she will be found.'

I nod, watching the teardrops falling on the blurry image of her sofa which, like the life I remember, all seems part of someone else, far away.

'In fact, I promise you, by the time you leave my attic, you won't have to think about her again.'

'Holly,' I look up at her, and down at what's left of me. The first burst of something closer to anger than sadness is clawing at my throat. 'I've sold my flat. My possessions are being sold or in storage. I have no savings left because I couldn't work. I still have her race-hate emails with "The opinions expressed in this email do not necessary represent those of the Royal Ornithological Society" at the bottom because she was sending them from work,' and then I was laughing, because it should be funny, and laughing even harder, to show her how funny it should be. Virginie had been made to apologise, an email in uncharacteristically fluent English cc-ed to the HR director. That was the day before she first followed me to my home. I only stopped laughing because all Holly would do was wait for me to calm down and do the sane thing. Just like I'd waited for Nick to do. 'I'll be looking over my shoulder for the rest of my life, Holly. I'm the monster in your attic...'

Holly shakes her head. 'It's yours. As long as you need it.'

'I will not destroy your life because she destroyed mine!'

'No.' A look of admiration, pride and triumph replaces her sympathy. 'I know you won't. You're already stronger than I've ever been. If a violent racist accounts clerk stole Tom, I'd be in your attic forever.' She's getting up, having seen Tom wave from the garden. 'Come on. Barbecue's ready.'

I'm about to follow, but something is eating at the corner of my thoughts. 'Holly?'

She stops, framed the glass doorway, fingers pressing the edges of the frame. 'Yes?'

'When did I tell you Virginie was an accounts clerk?'

A second passes, in which I know Holly is trying to keep her smile concealed. 'Come on outside. Tom can tell you more about this community we're part of.' She's first to run down to the bottom of the garden, give Tom a kiss on the cheek. 'My hunter-gatherer,' she's saying as I catch up.

Tom mimes being a caveman, with appropriate chimpanzee noises, then sees me watching, wipes his nose on his sleeve and stands almost imperceptibly straighter while pretending not to. I've never worked out why he thinks he has to be on his best behaviour with me, just because I've had a couple of collections of poetry published, let alone when I'm standing here in clothes I owned when I was seventeen that live in his attic and smell of the stagnant, forgotten years between.

Tom shows Holly something on his phone. I don't miss the look that passes between them, and I have a feeling I'm not supposed to. Then he goes back again to serving at a distance while Holly sets out our deckchairs.

'So. The jobs list,' I say. 'You were saying about joining your...'

'Cult?' Holly laughs, too quickly. 'Maybe see if there's something on the list you like the look of.'

She hands it over, and I scan the first-world problems with detached jealousy. *Research and change phone companies. Choose lawyer to make will. Deep-clean holiday house. Resolve hedge.* But each one could represent a threat as big as mine, a life on hold for a reason the outside world can't grasp from the list of ingredients. I'd never have realised that before. 'Holly?'

'Yes?'

'If you,' I ask quietly, 'or if Tom...I mean, you're nothing like them, of course you're not. But if one of you ever...'

She leans back in one of the three patio chairs, pats the one beside it. 'Fell in love with someone else?'

I nod, and sit on the grass beside her. I prefer the ground. It's always felt so much more real than chairs.

'If I stopped wanting Tom, or if Tom stopped wanting me, I'd rather that person moved on than die a thousand little daily deaths for the rest of our lives. I mean, not everyone literally kills each other, but it kills a lot of chances for real happiness, and what I'd call real love. It's not love to choose guilt and fear over courage and honesty.'

'Maybe it's different when you have children,' I say, hating myself for believing his excuses even now they've killed him.

Holly looks at me levelly. 'I'm not going to remind you Paul is in his twenties. But tell me this. Do you wish Mum and Dad had stayed together?'

'No.' I see in her eyes the same pictures that

flicker behind mine. 'Well, yes, in that I wish they'd stayed loving each other. I still think, you know, what might have happened if Mum had still loved him. She'd have found him that morning. Maybe in time. Not alone, flat on the bed, eyes wide open the way I did. As if he was trying to put off the heart attack by being calm. He died awake and alone and neither of us had forgiven Mum for stopping loving him and leaving him to die like that, even though we knew they were happier apart, lived real lives they never would have had if they'd stayed together. I wish they'd stayed wanting each other, but that's not the same thing.'

Holly controls a shiver. It's only then I remember she stayed outside the room. That I went in there alone. That I called the ambulance. That I was the one who wasn't afraid to look and keep looking until I knew how the story ended. 'But they didn't.'

'No.'

'So?'

'So no, I don't wish them on each other. I wouldn't wish a relationship like that on anyone.'

'Even Virginie?'

There's a hum beneath the silence. The jasmine and lavender are covered with bees, a constant, active blanket of movement, a community interacting in a constant current of activity and communication. Holly is thoughtful for a while. Then she asks, 'The son doesn't even live with them?'

'Toronto, I think.'

'Good luck, Toronto.' I almost smile again. A rare example of Holly worrying about something she can't control. 'Does Virginie have Nick's surname?'

'They were never legally married. She used it sometimes. This is the name her emails came from.' I pass her my disconnected phone. 'The police took the internet off it, but the emails she sent are still there. I had to copy and paste them because there were so many racist terms the police station's computer system wouldn't accept the emails. The emails kept bouncing back every time the sergeant tried to send them to himself from my phone.' Holly scrolls slowly, and I watch the bees in the lavender, a permanent hum of busy, constant activity. '"Gyppo not understand love... Satan himself... big-nosed slut from hell... the opinions expressed in this email do not necessarily reflect those of the British Ornithological Society." You couldn't make it up.'

I nod. 'She sent them from the office.'

Holly hands my phone back. 'Listen, Tom and I might come in late tonight, from working. We've got a job on. It just came up on the app and it's one I think I'll enjoy.'

'What's the job?'

'Admin.' Again, just too quickly. She nods at her phone. 'Joy, there's one thing more useful than understanding why someone does something, and that's knowing when to walk. And let them go to hell their own way.'

'It's a bit late for that, isn't it?'

Holly shrugs. 'It's always early for next time.'

It's only when I finally go upstairs to Holly's attic that I see she's texted herself screenshots of Virginie's emails. As I sit on the – my? – bed and look out of the – my? – window, I wonder how far loyalty goes, whether the things Virginie did to keep Nick safely in her life might have their equals in what Holly will do to keep me safely in hers.

If I do hear them coming back tonight, I will

turn over and choose to sleep. Tonight, I will let someone else do the rescuing. Tonight, I am going to learn not to need to know how the story ends.

Not the Fire,
Just the Light

The Vampire considers his reflection. His make-up brush – held in a steady, uniformly white hand – places a final, purple-tinted sweep through a black eyebrow. He glues and inserts one ceramic fang, then the next. The fact of a reflection aside, the Vampire is as perfectly vampiric as, were anyone there to witness, it would be obvious he thinks he is.

There is, of course, no witness.

I don't count.

They say the observed thing changes, but I really don't think he ever does. Granted, I'm biased. At dance school they told us to let go of the perfect. You could be poised, and careful, and see those safely in the mirror. Even dancers know chasing the perfect would only make you unhappy. That's all it could ever do.

But every year, he is here first.

The dressing room is empty but for the Vampire and the light: electric bulbs over the mirrors, splinters of rainbow from the tops of the stained-glass windows where this nightclub attic slices the former church in half. The place smells of make-up and hairspray, dust and expectation. The careful confidence of the Vampire is of one used to being watched, even in an empty room.

The dressing room door slaps the wall.

The Vampire breaks eye contact with himself, raises his gaze in the shaking mirror. His eyes meet those of the Skeleton Bride, her poise in the doorway a perfect stillness that still manages to communicate an internal shaking fury. Her make-up is as perfect as his, if careful is what we mean by perfect. Dance school taught us it was. And most who look at either her or him would forget the difference.

The Vampire raises an eyebrow, another deliberate gesture an observer – not me, I don't count – would suspect someone had once told him looked perfect. Someone did, of course. Me. I like to think he remembers.

The Skeleton Bride's scowl deepens, before she disappears, slamming the door shut harder than it opened. The door bounces on the frame and fails to close. The mirrors shake and rattle along every wall around the dressing room. Beyond the unshut door, down the corridor, stilettos and satin pound and swish, recede and disappear.

The Vampire returns to the violet and black of his eyebrow.

The room is as empty as it was, emptier for the waft of cold. This time, when the door blows open again, he does not look away from the mirror. But it's enough. The room is different. He lets himself know he is watched now. All I did was blow on this door, but it's the performance of the thing that matters. He'll let himself talk to me now. 'How are things?' he asks politely.

'Much as ever,' I reply. He still hasn't looked at me, but it's not because he can't see me, not anymore. Now it's because he's deliberately not looking where he knows I am. I see this, clear as if it were inked on the air. It's in his shorter strokes of the make-up, violet on black. 'You've seen her,' I say.

The Vampire looks briefly at the door the Skeleton Bride slammed. 'I hadn't. Not since last year.'

I nod, though I know he doesn't look. 'Another year.'

The Vampire, unseeing, mirrors my nod.

'Put the brush down.'

The Vampire dips the brush in the powder, raises it to his eyebrow again.

'It'll be too much if you keep going.'

'It'll be alright.'

'Maybe it will. But perfect is only going to get further off. Trust me, I recognize that place. I've been there.'

The Vampire turns from the mirror but his prepared words halt as his expression becomes, understandably enough, that of one who is seeing a ghost. It's not the green-grey of my skin in comparison with his brilliant white. Whatever's in my eyes is far harder to meet. 'Look man,' he says, and looks away. 'I really need to...'

'Of course.' I let him turn away, and step back towards my own corner where the mirrors meet.

'I mean, the show starts in an hour so...'

'I know,' I say.

'You know what it's like. I really need to...'

'I know. Ritual first. But we should talk after.'

He puts his hand out for the doorknob.

'I know,' says the Vampire.

'Or it'll only be another year.'

'I know.' He almost looks at me, for almost a second. 'We will.'

'You always say that.'

'I know. But... we will.'

Before he can reach for the doorknob again, it opens from the other side.

The Moth propels herself towards the mirror forehead first, focused and heavy as an animal following a scent. Her head is bowed over the cumbersome, fluffy oval of a body. Her antennae droop over her electric-green and jet-black fur. She straightens at the mirror and glares at the threadbare patch on her left pompom.

She looks up, at the Vampire watching her blow against her pompoms. 'I look like a mutated fairground toy,' she tells him in the mirror.

'It's not so bad,' the Vampire says.

'Mutated. Fairground. Toy.' But the Moth is smiling now, albeit into her fur. 'I swear this costume gets heavier every bloody year.' She unpacks the first few boxes of her make-up. Each box lands with a louder crash than the last. She doesn't look at the Vampire as she says, 'You saw her ladyship then?'

'Briefly,' says the Vampire.

'It's in your face.'

'So I hear.'

'Really? Who else said so?'

He barely hesitates. 'No one.'

More boxes, more crashes. The lid of one box comes off with an aggressive clack. 'You'd get over her better if there wasn't this to look forward to.'

'But there always is.' His face burns red under the make-up; it's quality stuff and I couldn't tell if I were looking, but anyone could feel it in the silence. Anyone who knew him, and heaven – not that I've seen it yet – knows we all do.

Another clack. 'Every fucking Halloween.' The Moth begins adding the final details of black over the green wash of her face, with a dainty paintbrush I don't recognize. At least some things do change from year to year.

The Vampire leans his weight against the counter, beside the Moth and his own abandoned brushes and greasepaint. I find things to convincingly occupy me, wandering in and out of the Vampire's view of himself in the mirror, giving them all the space it's in my power to offer. The Vampire looks from one mirror to the next, his gaze bouncing off me if ever it could become blocked by where I am; meeting his own eyes in each wall if he can, moving to another wall if he can't, always as if expecting to see something else that should be there instead. My own kit and make-up bags, perhaps, in my corner. However often he sees me, or doesn't see the evidence of me, he really doesn't seem to believe I've gone.

Finally he sighs, pushes himself off the counter, turns to the Moth. 'Does this look alright?'

The Moth regards him briefly, looks away fast, smiling at the question and muttering into her fur. 'Just get down there. You annoyingly perfect little shit.'

The Vampire offers a quick smile to the Moth, who drops her eyes and hides her blush by turning to the mirror.

The Vampire avoids being seen to see this, with a quicker, blanker look that he shares with me, before remembering he doesn't quite believe I'm here and looking away. He walks to the door, and closes it behind him with an efficient click. The Moth deflates as soon as the door shuts.

'Say something,' I tell her.

The Moth does not look up.

'Tell him.'

The Moth takes a cigarette lighter from the pouch concealed in her fur. She sinks into the chair the Vampire left, flicks the lighter on, and off, and on again.

'How will you feel if, in twenty years' time, he turns around and says, "Why didn't you tell me"?'

The cigarette lighter sparks and flickers in and out of life. The Moth watches the light.

I walk over to her and blow the flame out.

The Moth sighs.

'You know I'm here!' For some reason I'm shouting. I grab a make-up box, throw it to the floor though my hand never touches it. Whatever strength I find for this is the strength of pure belief. 'I know you know! I'm here!' Another box, another. The floor becomes a mess of make-up and still there is no sign the Moth sees the mess, or cares who is causing it.

'I miss you,' the Moth whispers.

My hand, almost unbidden, allows the next box to sink back to the counter unthrown. 'I know.'

'Her ladyship says beginners' call in—' The Vampire stops in the doorway, looks down at the contents of the Moth's make-up boxes covering the floor, a vibrant Halloween mess of neon, plastic and fur. He looks from where I and the Moth stand in the dressing room, to the dressing room mirror where there is only the Moth and himself. One white hand extends, and he encircles the Moth in an awkward embrace, his right hand pressing where my shoulder almost is. But he doesn't look at me. He looks at the mirror, where the same white hand presses against nothing.

'I can't see him,' the Moth whispers.

'I know,' says the Vampire.

'Tell me he's here.'

The Vampire holds her gaze in the mirror.

'Tell him we love him,' the Moth says to the Vampire.

'Tell her you love her,' I say the Vampire.

'What does he say?' the Moth asks.

The Skeleton Bride slams open the door again. Again, every mirror in the dressing room shakes.

'Um...' says the Vampire, breaking away too fast, jogging the Moth who, unable to disguise her tears, shuts her eyes.

'Beginners' call,' snaps the Skeleton Bride, her voice of ice and eyes of fire. If she has noticed the Vampire hugging thin air, that doesn't own the anger. 'Five minutes.'

'Um... I thought I'd uncloak on the spiral staircase this time? If we lock eyes over the bar—'

'No.'

'—and push towards each other through the crowd then the music has time to build—'

'Same as last year. It must be the same as last year,' she snaps. 'Everything must always be the same as it was last year. Everything. Always.'

'Alright. Alright. The same dance as last year. Same as every year.'

They follow the Skeleton Bride, and they fulfil her demands. They dance the story they have danced for seven years, appearing where they are expected, disappearing where they should.

I see it without being there, hear it from the dressing room. Until, after the same, beautiful tired dance, when the Moth has died her usual quiet death and the Skeleton Bride has dragged the Vampire back into hell while the Ghost – though now in the dressing room and not the stage – does nothing but whisper, circle and watch – then the dance floor is given over to the civilians. There's just a spotlight for me now, and they respond to me exactly as they would if they could see me. If I were still here. Then it ends. The professionals are free to find the shadows, slip out from under their perfect faces and venture, anonymous and free, into the dark.

Safely after midnight, when the dance floor is packed full of monsters, the Vampire walks back through the dressing room door.

I stop circling behind his chair and say everything that matters in four words. 'It needs to stop.'

'No.' He sits down, hard, in the safe familiarity of his dressing room corner.

'It does. This needs to be the last dance.'

The Vampire looks at his reflection, and only at his reflection.

'It's killing you all. That wasn't the deal. *I* was always the ghost. Not any of you.'

There is no sign the Vampire hears. He seems to have eyes only for his reflection.

But I don't choose to fall for that. What's left of me, of the Ghost, lays what's left of a hand on the Vampire's.

The Vampire turns from the mirror. He looks at his own hand on the counter, under what misty green reality there is of mine. Then he looks at his hand alone in the mirror, looks for the pressure of my fingers as if seeing that would allow him to believe in the fingers themselves. But his own are painted too white to register the pressure of ghost fingers, whether they are there or not.

'There will be other dances,' I say. 'You just have to stop this one first.'

'But what I did—'

'—is done.'

'If we stop the dance, you'll be gone.'

'Let me go.'

'No.' The mirror no longer far enough away, the Vampire shuts his eyes.

'I'm only here when you are.'

'No.'

'It's true. I fade when you three go. I don't remember anything from one year to the next. There's only been this dance. For seven years, there's only been this night. Nothing else. Not since the day I—'

'I still can't see him,' says the Moth.

The Vampire opens his eyes. We turn to the doorway.

'My sister,' I say to the Vampire. 'The only one

in the whole troupe of us who can open a door without a slam.'

'It looks like you're talking to no one,' the Moth tells the Vampire.

'You know who it is.'

'Tell him I love him.'

'He knows,' says the Vampire.

'Tell him anyway.' The Moth looks away from the mirror to the cigarette lighter in her hand.

'You've never smoked,' I say.

'He says you've never smoked,' says the Vampire. 'Why the lighter?'

She smiles. 'It's not the fire. Just the light.' She flicks it on, lets it burn this time. They watch the flame stand, quiver, disappear and stand again, throwing its temporary pattern among the neon bulbs and stained-glass rainbows. 'It wasn't your fault,' the Moth says, still looking at the flame.

The Vampire looks back to the mirror, taking refuge in his own eyes.

'Accidents happen, on stage and off,' the Moth says. 'You've got to let him go now.'

'It was my fault.'

'You know it wasn't.'

'I didn't see...'

'And you've got to stop letting *her* blame you.' Her eyes flick to the shut door; so do mine and the Vampire's, as if mentioning her name will summon the Skeleton Bride.

'She doesn't blame me for that,' says the Vampire.

'What, then?'

'I want her blame,' he says.

'Why?'

'Because he never wanted her,' I answer for him, though I know she can't hear. 'He wants someone to blame him. To convince him there was something he could have done. It's the only power left. Someone to call him monster.'

The Vampire gives no more sign of having heard than the Moth. We wait, the three monsters in the silent dressing room, and the two that appear in the mirror, watching the flame.

The music downstairs is turned off. The shouts and conversations are starting to fade. When the bar closes, there will be no more excuses. They will have to take the make-up off. And, unlike me, they'll have to find something underneath.

Wolf in
the Mirror

'The weirdest thing,' she says, twenty minutes late as usual, blowing in and crashing down in our usual booth, a cloud of library dust and Ocean Spray.

I hadn't glanced up when the pub door opened – never do – but I'd known. The pressure of the barman's eyes following her to me; quietly noting her cold cheeks kiss the air beside my bristled ones, the click of her tongue that was the only greeting and customary telling-off that I still wasn't shaving regularly, hadn't shaved regularly since Mary left.

My kisses, on the other hand, meet both her cheeks and, true to custom, she barely notices. Certainly my kisses never break the stream of news, especially now, this blazing contrast of living, breathing student life with the crust of a graduate session musician. Well, so it ever was; she was always waiting to be nineteen. I, at twenty-four, am what I too was waiting to be: the middle-aged man I already was at eighteen and aim to stay.

'I was at the BL,' she begins. My turn for a cluck of disapproval; the cliquey vulgarity of abbreviations. 'At my desk in the Reading Room, and my earring – in my ear – just fell out.'

She meets my studied look of eloquent pity. Her mop of black, coarse corkscrew hair is twisted into one of those ghastly topknots they all have now, and she's pointing at the silver and lime of the earring dangling from her earlobe. Hair pushed back, her skin is almost white, matching the winter sky over Richmond Green in the world behind her. Her back is to the outside world, so she's oblivious to how she matches it; eyes only for my disbelief. She's pointing at her earlobe, earring replaced, as evidence of how strange and right she is. 'Really, Rolly. It was the weirdest thing.'

I pick up the menu from the pub table. I hate this habit of calling me Rolly, the unthinking way she brings me closer than I want to be, a rhyme with her own name, an unthinking part of herself. Roland, incidentally, is a name I've never been ashamed of or sought to shorten. My birth in the Year of the Rat is a coincidence to which can be attributed nothing about my parents' feelings toward me. I tap the menu in the direction of the bar, fastidiously ignoring the landlord who's still watching us – her – and catch the eye of his latest junior instead. A nod acknowledges my order of our usual. I feel at home, just for a moment. 'By no stretch of the imagination, Molly Andrews,' I say, 'is a fallen earring in a library "the weirdest thing".'

She glares at me exactly as our mother would have done. She has the advantage of biology there, as well as the worldly one of inheriting the library that informed the glare. Our mother, hers by birth and mine by law, did not grow to hate me even as she grew to hate my father. I care little for either of the parents we shared and lost but offer them my thanks: without this girl to protect, to roll my eyes for, life would have been of little consequence.

Molly thanks the waitress as our sandwiches arrive. Prawn and cress, salad without dressing because I watch my weight and she dislikes the taste. This is the apex, the moment we settle here for everything to be the same for one solid lunch hour. A storm of resentment builds in me for the outside world, our separate lives, separate homes and everyone that shares them. I wish the world to shrink to the length and shape of a Tuesday lunchtime. I wish time and space to stay outside the window, to leave us alone.

'I want to tell you why I'm right,' she says.

I raise a cautious eyebrow.

'You remember when I promised you I'd always wear the little plastic things? The ones that go behind your ear so your earrings don't fall out?'

'Vividly.' The plastic things were a device of Mary's. I hit the pile of six bar mats I hadn't quite noticed I'd been building. They spin in the air and are caught, perfectly as always, in the straight line between my fingers and thumb. I am very good at precision. Anything I can take my mind out of. 'Repeatedly.'

'Well, I wasn't wearing them.'

'I have yet to detect the promised weirdness.'

'What?'

'Surely the absence makes it *less* weird that the earring fell, rather than more?'

Her eyes move to the window; she looks out

at the white and grey of Richmond Green for far too long.

'Molly?'

She jumps, looks at me as if she'd forgotten I were here.

'What is weird, please?'

She looks again at the outside world and I want to banish the whole lot of it. Then she looks at me. 'I felt it go, Roland. The second time it fell. I put it back in and I promise you it was pushed out – not even pushed. Slid. Slid out of the hole in my ear. I was sitting still. I was writing my essay. There was no movement. There's no other way my earring could have come out than someone deliberately sliding it.'

I try to rise above my squeamishness. I've always hated earrings, the concept of piercing. It's not the repetition of her stories about losing jewellery, although there are years enough of these and it suits me for her to think it is. It's the damn holes. The idea of anything being pushed, broken, hollowed – I don't like to hold a knife or a drill or a pair of meat-scissors for the vague thought it's now potentially possible I could do someone a mischief, there being nothing to physically stop me. Molly, though, loved piercings. The first thing

I knew about this little sister who arrived with her mother on my doorstep was that she adored anything silver. It brought out the kohl around her eyes. I try not to smile.

'You're asking if I believe in ghosts,' I say.

'Am I?' She releases the topknot, drops her hair back over her ears, as if it can protect her from memory, from possibility.

'I don't believe in anything that isn't there.'

'But there are things, aren't there? Other things... Things we don't understand?'

'Of course. But—'

'So something could be trying, couldn't it? Something could be there with me. Could choose to touch me, for some reason. Things do happen that we don't have terms for, don't they? Connections, coincidences, haven't you ever had the feeling that someone is more real than all the world that surrounds them? Felt there are things in earth and heaven too great for explanation?'

I try to look away from her. I really do.

'Don't you, Rolly? Aren't some things just too mysterious? Isn't that how it's supposed to be? Well, what if one reaches out for you, chooses you? What better definition could there be of "real"?'

Her eyes are wide, dark, pressing towards and away from looking into my own mind.

'Rolly?'

I stand too fast, trying to catch up with my own momentum as I walk badly towards the stairs, down to the only logical place for me to need to go. She must not know about the nerve she's touched.

The staircase is unusually cold, and unusually long. Richmond's history descends in badly-framed pictures above either bannister; there's a scent not unlike the one Molly drifts in with to the bowels of this building, of books and collected time. But something is different here today; the staircase seems to stretch. Something is wrong with my perception and I do not like it at all. Perception should not be permitted to drive reality; we evolved for better things. Her story has bothered me; that's irrational, but all. I am sensing what I don't believe in, and that is ridiculous.

I cannot protect her against what I do not believe in.

In the one long mirror that runs the length of the seven sinks and curls on to the edges of the walls, ten matching pairs of Roland Andrews splash water on their faces. They disappear into flannelled darkness as I dry my face with the first of a pile of hand towels. The pile topples. I don't dare look up from the counter where it's fallen. When I do I must meet my eyes in the mirror. I know what will be looking back.

'This must stop,' I tell myself aloud.

But it's never begun, replies a voice that seems to come from behind the collected, quiet green eyes I see every day in the mirror and am perfectly aware are not mine. Sometimes the eyes blaze yellow, most days they are dense algae. There has always been a wolf when I look in the mirror. I'm fairly sure he predates Molly and her mother. Sometimes he is concealed. But sometimes he is vivid, visceral, has more of me than I have of myself. Roland Andrews is a necessary camouflage technique, but the wolf is always in the mirror.

'It mustn't. I must not let it.'

Mustn't what?

'Be true.'

What mustn't?

'I must not.'

Thinking, saying, where's the difference?

'I must not.'

Say it. Say it to me. Say it again.

'I must not love her. Must not love her, must not, must not—'

My face darkens to grey, the green of my eyes glitters with something darker than tears. I can see him. My teeth are white as I open my mouth for air, my lips moving back and still I'm watching myself, all the time, my jaws working, my hair falling on my wet face, a desperate face that isn't mine at all but is the wolf, his green eyes, blood and hunger.

The movement of the door repeats behind the ten of us in the mirror. The man comes in just too quickly. We barely look at each other, but I'll remember his eyes. Aware, embarrassed. He goes into the furthest cubicle, and I look in the mirror again. But my connection with my own eyes has been cut, hollowed by interruption. The disguise has taken over again: Roland is mortal, cultured, nothing more than any man trapped between earth and sky. The moment of deeper truth has passed. The relief lasts as far as my shutting of the washroom door behind me. On the staircase, that cold is worse. It links somehow to the wolf's voice, but I cannot hear him. It's coming from the photographs. The stairs stretch up forever now. I am convinced that if I don't run for the top of them I will never see daylight again. As I run, the wolf's voice or mine screams through my mind as our life, Molly's and mine, no difference, flashes behind my eyes. *Must not love. You must not love—*

I run back upstairs and don't care that she sees me struggling to catch my breath. This is not the wolf panting, this is only me. I don't look at her but at the table. There are two glasses, one full of vodka and lime, the other of ice and a slice of lime.

'You bought me a drink,' I say.

'Only the usual.'

I don't look at her face. I can hear everything it would show me. I take the drink and thank her.

'Maybe it's being born on Halloween,' she says.

'What is?'

'Well, you. Something about the darkness. I always said at school my brother was a werewolf.'

'You are not my sister,' I tell her carefully.

I feel her looking up, though all I see is beer mats. The words themselves are a surprise, but the meaning is as familiar to her as to me. She looks at me as if calculating my reality, my proximity and my separateness, as if for the first time. 'No,' she says. 'I am not.'

I can see my face in the pub window in the growing darkness, and there he is, the wolf who watches me out of my eyes. I hold that gaze for once; dare to ask him what he wants. I dare to ask him why.

The window becomes a mirror in the growing darkness. From time to time we catch each other's eyes in the glass. Then we look away, and look again, watching each other watching the rain.

Green
Lady

'And this,' says Dad, 'is the very, very important bit.'

He leans forward, eyebrows in a deliberately serious scrunch. But there's a twinkle in his eye, like we share a secret. Which we do, of course. We always did.

Dad pushes the arms of the corkscrew down. He looks at me, making sure I'm concentrating. I nod back. He puts his other hand around the wide green skirt that makes up the bottom half of the corkscrew. The round silver face has its same old childish, lightly evil smile. I used to hate that smile. Mocking me, she was, for never being able to work her out. But I was used to her. We grew up together, that green lady and me. Only she gets to stay on her safe, happy shelf in the kitchen, forever. I never thought I'd end up jealous of the green lady.

'Check the foil is already off the top, of course,' says Dad, a little sharply, like he knows my mind is wandering. Then, lighter, 'Make sure she's sitting comfortably.' He squats the green lady over the cork of the wine bottle. 'The important thing is to be firm but gentle. Don't hurt her, don't surprise her. Otherwise she'll be all flustered and you'll get bits of cork in the wine.'

The green lady's arms go up, gradually, like she's cheering in slow motion. I'm struck by how easily Dad does this, how much slower he consciously takes it so I can follow what he never even needed to think about. A white gold eternity snake, the wedding ring that was Mum's first design at art college, curls around his finger. There's just a suggestion of bottle green paint in his cuticles and stubble, from the latest theatre set being painted in the workshop that week.

Then Dad freezes. A lime rectangle appears across him and our kitchen. *Mum* proclaims the rectangle. *Home.* It's accompanied by my favourite ringtone – *Star Trek: The Next Generation* – that I downloaded ages ago for family calls. But the familiarity of it is hollow now. I look up from my phone screen where our kitchen is, to the kitchen I'm alone in. The counter I'm perched at is bare, encircled by industrial style worktops, beige, grey, none of the colours of life. If I look through the door I can see the beginning of the pokey student hall that stretches on forever, adjoining twelve strangers behind twelve shut doors. It's the opposite in every way to our cheerfully awkward, quirky old bungalow. If I could only crawl into the frozen screen, out of this cold and anonymous new world that's too big and too small at the same time. But even though I can't imagine "home" ever meaning anywhere but that bungalow, and even though Mum's calling me from it right now, I don't want to answer.

The video clip of Dad is almost grey under the lime rectangle and the bright red and dark green of the two spots: green to answer Mum's call, red to avoid the call and go back to the video of Dad. I don't care which I do. It doesn't seem to matter. The options don't even seem like different colours. Neither option means hearing Dad's real voice, ever again.

But the right thing to do is to answer, so I might as well go with that that. I'm not the only one who misses him, even if I'm the only one in this kitchen. 'Hello?' I hear my voice say. It sounds exactly like me, like I always have whether I want to or not. Calm, clipped, a bit underwhelmed. Like nothing has changed: a perfect parody of being the same person I always was. I'm doing a perfect impression of me.

'Sian.'

My mum always says the name of whoever she's calling, not her own name. It doesn't matter whether she's talking to her own child or the gas board. I listen to her drop my name into the silence like a pebble into a pool. I picture the rings spreading out, wait for them to dissipate before I reply, 'Yes.'

'All going well.' It isn't the question it's supposed to be. It's a statement, demanding confirmation not information. Most people would ask how your first month at university has been, instead of tell you. But not Mum. Mum doesn't do questions. Mum only does certainties. Gives you the cue, so you can come back at her with the right answer. And of course that habit's got a lot worse since the greatest certainty in her life has gone.

'Fine,' I say.

'I would have come if you'd wanted.'

That's one certainty that really does happen to be true. And I'm not lying when I answer, 'I know that, I know you would.' I'm just leaving out how very much I didn't want her to.

I don't blame Mum for the false certainties. It really isn't that. I don't blame her for the way she never said anything remotely pessimistic about Dad's condition and diagnosis, nothing to even slightly prepare me for how wrong she was in her life maxim that everything was going to be a) for the best, and b) alright. I don't blame her that I had to learn how very, very wrong the ideas that shaped my mind for my entire eighteen years had been all the time, while simultaneously trying to learn how to say goodbye to my dad; learning that goodbye is a process that starts while everything still seems almost normal, when denial is the only realistic option, when they're still apparently absolutely fine. That the before, when and after of losing someone you love means the weeks and months go on and on and you're still saying goodbye and still haven't even begun saying goodbye yet. I'm never going to burden Mum with how much I wish she'd protected me with even a little bad news, instead of trying to protect me from it.

'But it's going alright?' I hear it, I'm pretty sure I do: the question mark creeping in at the edge of her voice.

'Yes,' I say. I hope it's soft enough, not too much like a snap, like an order. I don't find soft any easier than she does. That's why I needed Dad, and why she did too. Dad, translating the world we both exist into something less cold, something more gently and pleasantly alive. Something that wasn't always such an intensely big deal. 'Honestly. It's good here. It's fine.' None of that's a lie. Not really. It'll be true soon. All of it. I'll make it so.

'Are the videos... are you watching the videos?'

'Yes.'

'Are they helping?'

'Yes.' I wipe my eyes and thank God Mum doesn't know how to FaceTime.

'That's good.'

'Yeah.' Dad always helped me do practical things. He knew I struggled, just like Mum struggled. Things that happened two thousand years ago, me and Mum are great at. We know the history, and the mythology, and the signs on ancient pots and cutlery that tell you about the makers and the owners and the composition of the clay. Things that happen under our noses are more of a mystery, like where the scissors are (in the usual pot on the kitchen counter) or what the difference is between the oven and the grill (still unclear), and when you use one (fish fingers) or the other (baked potatoes) and when it doesn't matter (chips).

Mum is Professor Emeritus at her university but in the kitchen she never got beyond being a bad apprentice. Before Dad's diagnosis, he'd always done all the cooking. It was Dad who budgeted before and after all the bills went out, Dad who googled and booked family holidays. There was no question who wore the apron in our house. It was a black apron, with the Starship Enterprise on it and "Make it so" in a speech bubble coming from the saucer section – which always slightly irritated Dad because Captain Picard, whose catchphrase it was, would normally be on the Bridge and that was in the other section of the ship. Dad isn't wearing the apron in this video because it's only a wine bottle, but it was really clear in the spaghetti one.

I remember when I first watched the final episode of *The Next Generation*, Dad shaking his head and saying, "There'll never be another captain like him." I haven't dared watch *Star Trek* again.

'I limit myself to one video clip a day,' I tell Mum. I hope I make it sound like a choice, like I'm okay. The truth is I'm desperately rationing Dad's videos. None of them are more than three minutes, because Dad and I worked out that was the best for getting the greatest number of different practical little video clips on my phone. I say "we", really that was Dad too. There's a few more of them on my iPad, and some up in the cloud, but then Dad made a joke about soon being up in the cloud that made me cry so much he put the rest on hardware.

Anyway, if I limit myself, and don't get greedy, it'll be like I can have a new conversation with Dad every day until the Easter holidays at least. I might have to start missing out weekends, because university terms work as semesters and I want to be sure they'll last until the end of this one. I don't tell Mum this because she always snorts at the word "semesters" because it's an Americanism. But I always agree when Dad says – when Dad said – who cares whose idea it was if it means you get longer holidays?

'Which one is today?' Mum asks, and this time it really is a question. I guess it's safe to not know the answer to which video your daughter is watching half way across the country.

'Opening a bottle of wine,' I tell her.

'With the green lady?' There's a smile in the question.

'Yes.' There's a smile in my answer too, at the confirmation I didn't know I needed: that my memories are real, are shared between real people, are not just in my phone and me. That there's a world beyond this empty kitchen where I haven't even bothered to turn on the light; that I'm here, I exist in a present that has plenty of room for the past and even, perhaps, the future. "I'm not watching them in order. The videos. It's a bit more urgent than that. We've got a dinner party at the weekend. I want to be able to open a bottle of wine and not have to ask someone else to do it.'

'Who's we.' Back to the questions that aren't questions. I roll my eyes, tell her it's just me and two of the girls from my floor, work out how to play the video on silent so I can run the green lady back and forward, watch her twisting in silent, repetitive circles.

As I wind forward and back, and the green lady does too, it's like I can hear the words Dad said after we switched the camera off. "Go for it," was what he said after I'd stopped crying at the cloud joke. "Spending three years learning about the thing that is most interesting to you is amazing, Sian. It's your job to learn interesting things! For three whole years!" I was still snivelling a bit, but I nodded, acknowledged that technically he was absolutely right while implying that that wasn't the point at all. He read me loud and clear. "I don't want to say you have to go," he said, re-reading my A Level results and trying not to beam. "You do have a choice. You could stay here, forever if you really wanted to. But new is good, Sian. People, places, jobs, relationships, they need to renew themselves, shed skin, grow beyond their old limits, engage with whatever is happening now. Because alive things keep growing. Whether you want them to or not." He was looking at his fingernails but I knew he was talking about the cancer.

"But I want you to be there."

He put both his hands on my shoulders. They smelt of woodchip and that stuff you wash paint brushes in. "I am."

'You didn't used to like her,' says Mum. It's almost like she can tell I've started the video again, silently. But Mum could never find speakerphone, let alone tell when I was on it.

'Who?' I ask.

'The green lady.'

'No.' I stop the video, take her off speakerphone, put the mobile back on my ear. 'I thought she was laughing at me.'

'I thought she was laughing at me too.'

'Really?' I can't help smiling at that. No one would dare laugh at Mum, least of all a corkscrew.

'Oh, yes. That daft smile of hers. "Silly old Laura, can run a university department but can't open a bottle of wine".'

'Would you like me to send you one of the videos?' It's out of my mouth before I've consciously thought of it. I'd never have considered sharing Dad's videos. Yet somehow now I've said it, it seems like the obvious thing to do. I almost like the idea.

Nothing happens long after the rings have dissipated around the words I dropped into the silence. Eventually, Mum says, 'Yes.' Then there's even more silence, and I don't break it because if she's not going to let me know she's crying there's absolutely no way I'm going to let her know I am. 'Thank you, Sian.'

'Okay,' I say.

'Although,' then there's a silence that she's trying to make sound like a emphatic pause rather than an emotional one. 'He did make them for you.'

'I'm okay with sharing them with you, Mum. Honestly.'

And I am. I go back to speakerphone and find the next video. This one has the black apron with the little Starship Enterprise with "Make it so" on the front. 'I think it's stuffed mushrooms next,' I say.

'I'm posting you the *Star Trek* apron,' she says.

I pause the video, put the phone back on my ear. 'No,' I say.

'Oh. Well. Alright.'

'No, I don't mean no. I mean, exams are over in a couple of weeks. Maybe I could come down at the end of the month? Are you free that weekend?'

There's another of those silences.

'Mum?'

'Make it so,' she says.

Ash's
Creatures

The hairbrush rests where my ankles cross, the floor tiles cold beneath my suit trousers. I've stopped wondering how long I've sat here, my eyes following the stranglehold of tight electric-blue hair around the jet-black bristles. I've not touched the hair. I am starting to wonder what I expect will happen if I do. Time will begin flowing in reverse, perhaps? Unwind my very presence in this house until my predecessor instead of myself is holding this hairbrush, standing where I sit on this bathroom floor, brushing these strands from a head that never knew I existed or would exist, while creating the reality in which I sit, clutching their ashes?

Of course I do not think that. I do not think that at all.

But neither do I touch the hair.

There's a turn of the handle, a grunt of quiet apology, the clack and shuffle of Eliza's felt slippers on the aging carpet, down the gently creaking stairs to the pile of undergraduate essays she is perpetually marking at the living room table. No sound this house makes is a surprise to me anymore. But that doesn't mean it isn't keeping secrets.

The brightness of the hair is astounding. I don't believe I understood how electric could be called a shade until now. It was the brightness I saw, the colour and not the object it clung to, as I knelt to slot the pile of neatly-folded towels onto the shelf and caught sight of this relic, this accidental ghost, forgotten in its corner as one era of this house slipped into the next; awoken, returning to haunt me at the very moment I enact my first gesture of belonging. As if, left at the back of a cupboard, abandoned by someone too tall or busy or rich (I suspect all three) to remember and retrieve it, it is still vibrant with the spark of a life never meant to touch mine.

My first gesture of belonging is comprehensively upstaged now, laughable even if only behind the privacy of a locked bathroom door and my own mind. But even those make it more than real enough. I cannot unread this sign the house and its former occupant have given me, just when I began to think of this house as home. Yet for all that it is a strange, small victory thrill: this physical piece of a past I sense myself living under yet only learn about from Eliza's occasional, selective translations.

Other people's pasts have always taken on a magical quality; partly akin to fame, partly akin to death. I blame my father and our summer fossil-hunting trips for my addiction to that feeling: the exact same chill creeping outward from the back of my neck; that same sense of touching time, of placing a finger on something that no one has held or seen since it formed and became itself, before the finder existed in the world where they would, eventually, touch it.

Not since finding the hairbrush have I made a single movement, given time the slightest permission to start moving forward again.

I sit on the cold floor between my choice of future and someone else's past.

I cannot tell Eliza. She does not deserve this unkind and unnecessary reminder, does not deserve her sense of loss rekindled simply to assuage my own selfish guilt.

This is just a hairbrush. It will be discarded as such.

But Eliza's past is not mine to throw away. I cannot do that either.

This not my ghost to lay to rest.

~

She had settled herself in the armchair by the window, the soft, unshowy brown of her hair matched and mirrored in the felt of the cushions and the dark oak of the table and bookshelves turning uniform, sparkling gold in the late afternoon sunlight; a perfect window box of perfect irises behind her, outside the perfect sash window open to the perfect lane stretching down the perfect hill, made all the more unbearably perfect by the marmalade cat which leapt, purring, into her lap the moment she'd returned from opening the door to me before she asked, quite unaware she was the perfect illustration of the answer, 'And what attracts you to living around here?'

'Everything.' My reply was instant, and so artlessly honest it almost made me jump. 'Well, the job, obviously. That came first. The university. Initially.' Yes, that was better. Aloof, mature, safely unconcerned by the outcome, too old for belief in the magic that my voice when left to its own devices had jumped to acknowledge. 'I'm new to the town; it's not as if there's any rush. The bed-and-breakfast is perfectly suitable... I hoped the right place would find me rather than racing myself to find it.'

A small breeze blew in the scent of the jasmine bush outside the window filling the room. The cat rolled over in her lap.

'However...' I managed.

'However?' She smiled, patient and interested and perfectly at home in this perfect home. I opened my mouth again to see what would come out.

'Well. I don't want you to think I'm... because I'm certainly not...' Desperate? Naturally I was desperate. I was fighting my mouth's upper-middle-class reflex action of telling her to please take all the time she needed, that I completely understood there would be others. If I encouraged her to take longer, to decide at leisure between applicants, then I deserved everything I wouldn't get. I had to override my infernal good manners, no matter how hard they fought to undermine my objectives. 'I must

say the lady who runs the place is somewhat...
overzealous.'

She said nothing, but her smile seemed to read
a story in my eyes, and to encourage me to tell one.

'It's the breakfast, rather than the bed, that
presents the quandary.' I scratched my ear, for
something to do with my hands. 'I'm a lifelong
vegetarian and every morning when I – politely
– refuse a full English breakfast she replies, "No?
Oh!" Exactly the same shocked tone, every
morning. I assure her that coffee and toast are
all I need or want. Yet every morning my choice
is a fresh afront.'

'She disapproves?'

'Of vegetarians? Not in so many words.'

'Of you, then?' Here was a lack of
embarrassment I rarely saw, at least in anyone
looking at me. It was an acknowledgement of
the existence of the question everyone usually
wants to ask. She hadn't started with asking my
name, which was most people's weapon of
choice, and which provided a pleasing dearth of
clues – my name being almost as androgenous
as my face.

'Not in words, not at all. But to forget so
repeatedly...'

'Yes. You're right.' There was knowledge in it; memory. She had been part of this story before. After all, this story was not only mine.

I yearned to ask her background, demand an itemisation as everyone else usually did of me. It was quietly enthralling, to be tempted to take the enemy's part, to be tempted to ask her the questions that were usually mine to ward off.' 'I think she's just the mothering type. The type that needs to mother whether mothering is warranted or not. That will mother one into needing mothering. I don't respond well to...'

'Mothering?' A quiet, teasing eyebrow; the lady or gentleman had protested too much.

'Oversolicitousness.' I only looked back into her eyes; it was beneath the words, 'I admit it would be something of a rescue.'

'Perhaps for us too,' said the girl. Senior to me as she was within the department, and perhaps by the odd year or two, I couldn't help thinking of my future landlady, as I would anyone my age, as a girl rather than a woman. As the uniformly white-haired researchers I spent my days around thought of me, so I thought of myself: a youth. It made for an over-conscientiousness of time on my side, a sense of comparative wealth of the stuff to live through before I would turn from my larvae stage to become one of those ghostly white butterflies. Compared with them, and there was only them to compare, my every day had a convincing stretch of forever. But a day like this, with the reality of a world my own age I wanted to be part of, reminded me how very much alive I was. The pressure of it was more than I could bear.

'It would? How long has the room been vacant?'

'Not long.' There was a distance in her face now. 'The situation had become,' she stroked the marmalade cat and looked with distant familiarity at the peaceful, perfectly sunny world beyond her window, 'far too comfortable.'

'You and...? I'm sorry,' I addressed the cat. 'I don't know your name.'

The cat regarded me with glassy, unapologetic eyes.

'This is Robertson. No, not us.' She smiled, but it was a smile that was a choice, a rejection of the pain that was itself not yet a choice, nor anywhere near becoming one. Whatever happened, it had happened recently. 'Myself and your predecessor. Far too...comfortable.'

At her use of "predecessor", when no formal decision had been reached, my heart seemed to lift the eaves, fill the yet-unseen rooms with joy at whatever was to come, merely because it would come. Perhaps that was why it took against me, if it did: my spirit of unaffected, unconcealed appreciation did not meet with its cool reserve. But the joy was brief: one look back into her eyes and I saw in mentioning my predecessor she had returned to a past she wasn't free of, that I and Robertson and this room and this day had been relegated to future ghosts. Yet I belonged here. I was already more content, more comfortable in her silence than in any conversation I'd ever had.

'Not that I have any problem with comfortable.' She was trying to believe in the present again, rowing against the current of her own thoughts. The past was still far more real than I was. 'Only, it can be something of an antithesis, can't it.'

'To?'

'Life.' And there was something in the way she laughed at the word, the way she stroked Robertson, the way the animal's back in return seemed to follow the pressure of her palm moving over it as if there were a concealed magnet sliding along between fur and skin. But we'd known each other barely half an hour. It was not personal; I had not the ammunition of time for jealousy of my predecessor yet.

'You don't mean... I'm so sorry. Do you mean my predecessor is no longer...?'

She looked up, present again, and laughed. 'Oh, no, nothing like that. I have no reason to believe that Ash is anything other than alive and well.'

'Oh,' I said. *Ash*, I thought. 'Good.' Because even then I had started to sense that it wasn't.

'It's just that if you don't grow, you stagnate,' she said, still running her magnetic fingers along Robertson's back, with a fluency suggesting she didn't believe a word she was saying. 'Ash was the first to recognise that, though it came as no surprise to me. And there's no point in stagnating in a university town, where everyone's at the beginning of everything. If you're too comfortable in your enclosure you stop shedding skin, stop growing into the latest version of yourself.' She smiled, no doubt to show me she took lightly the weight of what she'd said. 'It wasn't healthy for either of us, being so content. We were far too young for that.'

'Perhaps you can still be friends,' I said, stupidly. 'It's often the best thing. I'm friends with many of my...' I trailed off because of her face. Even willing stupidity can be neutralised in the presence of quiet, self-assured truth. That wouldn't, her face said before she needed to, be the best thing for anyone. Ash, then, whoever Ash was, had not entirely left. At least, not sufficiently for my already-forming purposes, for the satisfaction of the scratchings of jealousy already beginning at the back of my mind.

'Anyway,' she continued, 'move in as soon as you like. A true gentleman shan't resent being rescued.'

The words "true" and "gentleman" as much as "move in" made me look straight into her eyes, something I do not find easy or natural. She did not look away, which I would learn was unusual for her too.

Had she said "real man" I would have seen a question, a challenge, my answer deciding how I would be received in the world, which of its boards I would been pinned on. The excellent thing about the job at the university seemed to

apply at my home-to-be as well: a profound...
more than acceptance, a lack of curiosity. I'd
never spent so long anywhere without being
asked whether Harry was short for Harriet or
Harold. Once or twice someone seemed about to
ask, displayed the regular precursors to the one
question even the highest-minded artists and
scientists feel they must grapple, to stick their
mental pin in you, apply you to the right board.
She hadn't, and we'd been talking for a full
twenty minutes. She understood who I chose to
be, read my body language, my choices, knew
that for some of us aesthetic spoke clearer of our
reality than the biological and social obligations
I was still learning to overcome.

'Eliza, by the way.' She held out her hand.

'Eliza,' I repeated, shaking it with both of
mine. Her first name was the last thing I learned
the day we decided, without either of us having
to ask or to offer, that we would live together. I
opened my mouth again at the door to ask her
another question, realising just in time there
were no words for what I wanted to identify in
the perfect bookshelves, the pale green walls and
sprinkling of art and pot plants: what was it
about this place I knew was so right that I felt I

had to have seen it before? A recollection in reverse was what I seemed to have found, a memory of a life yet to come, as surely mine as those that went before. If I opened my mouth to tell that much truth, even I would doubt myself.

But at the last moment, when I reached back over the doorstep to shake her hand again, I confessed anyway. 'I feel as if I know you. Or as if you know me.'

She smiled, her quiet green eyes full of strange certainty. 'I do, I think.'

It is no more to say you believe or disbelieve in love at first sight than it is to say you believe or disbelieve in any other instant, irrational decision within the conscious and subconscious mind of a human being. Of course any one of us can make an instant, irrational decision. And I was perfectly aware that I had. I walked off whistling, without any awareness I'd left without giving her my name until I reached the corner. All I knew was she had looked at me and seen the person in front of her, been intrigued by who – instead of what – I was: cared what was true, not what was real; an un-worded acceptance of who I was and who I chose to be. That was why I looked at her and saw a home.

She hadn't asked my biology. She hadn't even asked my name. As a result, she knew me.

'Harry!' I shouted from the corner, thumping my chest so she knew I meant myself. 'Harry!' At the time I didn't even know if she heard, but I will always remember how she smiled.

~

I could throw the whole thing away: hair and brush and curiosity alike. Even if Eliza isn't still grieving for this woman – or man? Am I so great a hypocrite as to take long hair and a name like Ash as proof of a gender, proving my thoughts as narrow as those of who I despise, assigning sex by aesthetic? – and for whatever happened or could have happened between them, she does not need to be put through such a sharp reminder of her barely-settled feelings simply so that I can look my reflection in the eye, appease my self-image and call it my conscience.

But even that comparison makes me grip the handle of the brush a little harder. Ash is a mystery, a kind of which I am used to being on the other side. I thought I knew about such things, but my own mystery is clear to everyone who meets me. So clear they think it an invitation to solve it: examine the pieces and come to a decision, whether I am or am not the man I choose to be. Others accept, or respect, or ignore rather than try to solve me. But the mystery now in my hands is not mine, is one that affects me and over which I have no control. Before, I had looked on her conversation about Ashley as a photograph of a time before we met, without assigning jealousy or fault or betrayal. Before, I would have laughed my invisible laugh at anyone desperate enough to ask me what I longed to ask of Ash, and cannot ask. I am a footnote to a story I've not been told.

I could unwind the hair, bury the strands in the food recycling bin on the kitchen counter, give the brush away to a charity shop. That would be logical, straightforward. Kinder, in so very many ways, than bringing it to her attention, making it her choice and her problem when it need be neither.

Or I could – and I tell myself clearly this is not a serious option – keep it. Hide this artefact in the very bedroom I've been so busily claiming back from its own past. Bring it right back in. With every thought I grip the handle harder and harder. It is probably my imagination that the blue is filling the air, that a fast and glittering zigzag of electricity passes from the hair through my body. The thrill on the back of my neck from finding the fossil is nothing to the possibility of looking at the live creature, eye to eye.

Real or not, in the moment the strange electricity flows through me I see a face, and shut my eyes to see it clearer.

I have never seen the face before and I know exactly who it is. I still don't know if Ashley is a girl or a boy, but like Eliza knew, when she looked at me, who I was, that I was part of the future whatever my name was, I know that I am looking at the past standing in my way.

'Who were you?' I ask the face in the safety of my mind, and do not care whether I am speaking aloud in my own world, which of us is haunting the other. Perhaps if someone haunts you long enough, you get to haunt them right back.

~

She stopped in my bedroom doorway, gripping the two cups of tea so hard her fingers turned as white as her face, and staring into the newly laid out room. 'Harry, how did you know?'

'Know what?' I asked, if only to prove to myself I did not feel it coming, when in truth the silence screamed with it.

'It's just... the layout. It's exactly as it was when...with Ash here.'

'Sensible Ash.' I stood, demonstrated the ease and direction of the light on the table by pulling back the nearer curtain. 'If you need a reason to be unafraid it's easily come by.' If I was mansplaining, performing my chosen identity warts and all, it was a price we could both afford for this display of how unthreatened I am, how little we should need to creep around the past. Nothing much had been said, or needed to be when I arrived. I had simply returned with my one suitcase and two boxes of watercolours; I'd unpacked, laid out the room as made it feel like mine, or simply like itself. The view from the desk and the light thrown on it from the window were perfect: for writing; for painting; for seeing out and not being seen; for anyone passing behind me to register in the movement of shadows. Ashley for separate reasons (some kind of art? I'd already found a threaded needle, silver and black, stuck in the carpet under what was now my desk but Eliza changed the subject rather than tell me what for), I for my oils and watercolours and clay. 'The sun just rises and sets every day on me at the same angle it did on...' Her? Him? Why did I of all people need to know so badly? 'On Ashley.'

'You're right. Of course you're right.' She passed me one of the mugs and leaned her shoulder against the doorframe as we drank our tea, until I remembered the power was mine and asked her to sit.

The only chair was at the desk. She hesitated, looking for too long at the chair. I leaned a hand on the bed as I drank my tea and talked idly of watercolour technique, in a way that probably interested neither of us. It was easy to see her seeing her ghost sitting there, and I didn't comment when she sat instead beside me on the bed. In other circumstances, I would feel guiltily pleased, subconsciously encouraged. But all I thought, deliberately looking away from the empty chair, was how a person of the height and confidence I was convinced Ash had would have sat in that chair, how now it was empty we still both felt Ash watching me, judging my skill and triple-bluff of confidence beside Eliza.

Something rustled against the bed at the side

by the wall. The sheets were untucked in that spot and, unthinkingly, I slid my hand down the side to straighten them. I delicately reversed, my fingers disappearing into fur. Unpleasant only by its unexpectedness, I drew away my hand. 'What's that? Has Robertson killed something?'

'It's alright.' She couldn't possibly see from where she sat, but the certainty in her voice told me even this was part of an ongoing story in which I was still barely a footnote. 'It's just one of Ash's creatures.'

I reached back, with more care and dread now that I knew something was there, considering my reaction before any inkling of whatever I would see.

The body lurking down the side of my bed was perfectly preserved; a beautifully expressive, anatomically correct mouse, balanced between the cute and the well-observed, down the side of the bed. 'It's...' I could almost say it was good. 'It... lacks nothing, but life. I take it your friend was a taxidermist?'

'Harry, I'm so sorry...' I turned the ghost's first offering around, looking at it from all angles. 'I thought we cleared the room out perfectly...'

'Do I look the type to stand on a chair, lift my skirts and scream at a mouse?' I smiled, as if to put her at her ease, and was surprised to watch her blush, making me play my words back to myself and blush in return. I hadn't even noticed there was anything to read into us both sitting on the bed. 'This one's beyond the point of doing harm.' I hope she thought me sure of this, whether or she thought I meant the mouse.

'I wonder if Ash meant to leave it. A parting gift.' We had not moved from the edge of the bed, but were facing towards each other now, instead of away.

'A gift? Yes. Perhaps.' Or a parting challenge. A claim. 'Most people ask me what Harry is short for,' I say as conversationally as the sad and jealous fury at the depth of my soul allows, the need to be recognised as unrecognisable. 'A way to avoid offending me by asking what they really want to: *girl or boy*? As if you can't see anything in a person if you can't see that. Depending on my mood, sometimes I answer. To which I add a benevolent expression, forgiving, as if it knew neither of us has chosen this.'

'And you want to ask me if Ash was a man or a woman.'

'I admit... I'm tempted.'

'When someone asks you, do you say, "Why do you want to know"?'

'Yes. I recognise that anger, that principle-driven need to know why the information matters, when identity, truth, will never be the answer. We merely want our performance notes, our cues. But the answer is because of you,' I say. 'Because I want to know your precedents. Because I want to see how far I am out of my role, as well as my league.'

'If that's all you're worried about then you don't need to care about the answer.' She's still looking at me, and I'm stereotypical man enough to take that invitation to lean closer. 'All I've ever wanted in a *person* I could love, for them to want me for who, not what, I am.'

Whatever point I think I'm making, I lean over and place the taxidermy monstrosity on the mantelpiece and make sure it's facing us: the past can damn well watch me instead of the other way around.

I let it watch us talk, and then I let it watch us kiss, and then as I stand in the space that Ash gave up before me, that if Ash were not gone I would never have entered, and I let it watch me remove my clothes, reveal my body, answer all the wrong questions and see what truth it makes of me beneath. I suppose what I'm doing is telling the room it shouldn't have to choose between the present and the past. I suppose I thought the house would understand. It was sending the messages I received. I was not alone in interpreting the signs; something was reading the ones I sent back.

~

I leave the bathroom only when the front door shuts. It's Eliza's late teaching evening, and I'm alone for five safe hours. Time enough to select a reality to move forward in.

I gently unwind the electric blue hair from the brush, half expecting a jolt of current. All I feel is human hair.

Part time hours in the university's library have given me ample time, and the room in Eliza's home ample space, to live in my head. Why should we seek only the shallow and temporary fulfilment of the real world, that sees only the patina, not the clay of our identity, of self? A strong base gives you courage, to not want a wider world. The more time I spend here, shaping the present, the better I became acquainted with my own daily and nightly rhythm of my thoughts and needs and satisfactions, the less the shallowness of the "real" world competed. Unnecessary things and people fell away. I was left with the perfect clarity of the present. I was simply and perfectly myself. Her love was the permission to need beyond this house. To settle for perfect. I could not begin to imagine how Ash had resisted the opportunity to settle for perfect.

'I know you're here,' I tell the empty flat. 'Leave us alone now.'

These days everyone is a witch, a time traveller. Just add a name to a colour of hair and I could know as much about Ash as I do about the woman who sleeps on the other side of what is now my wall and once was Ash's. How many blue-haired Ashleys have tagged themselves? It would be the easiest thing in the world to bring up this stranger's social media profile on a screen and know a little more of the truth.

But as I hold the hair over the bin, I hear a voice call me from my own room. 'This life has fallen into your lap,' she says. I'm sure it's a woman, though her voice is as deep as mine is light. 'It doesn't owe you anything.' The voice is naturally deeper than mine for reasons stronger than our bodies, instinctive strength that makes me instantly feel I'm losing some undeclared competition. 'Why are you desperate for someone's permission to take it?'

I stand in the edge of my own doorway. It's not that she's exactly as I imagined her, but seeing her makes every piece fall into place. The woman sitting on the bed is around our age, with blue hair, and painstakingly kohled, unapologetic eyes.

'You can't be here,' I say. 'You're not dead.'

'Prove it,' she answers. I would not have imagined a smile that smug on any face Eliza cared for. As such, I can only believe this is really happening.

'That you're not dead?' I ask.

'Or that I'm not here.' She also is too imperfect for me to have imagined her. My jealousy would not have let me off so easily. There is something coldly, unapologetically real, something making the best it can in her imperfectly straightened hair, the cheap foundation that is drying her skin. There is too much that is imperfect, hurried and maintained, too much that exists in the confines of time. There is nothing eternal about her. She is as temporary as anyone I've ever seen.

I turn the hairbrush over in her lap. Scarlet gothic italics scream its brand-name on jet-black plastic, as familiar as it is strange. I always liked that brand. I like to think that would have been my brand if I'd been that kind of a girl. If I'd wanted to be any kind of girl. I decided against both, but on other paths, and courageous versions of them at that, this would have been my brand.

But Eliza is more real to me that anyone or anything that predates her; her apparent preferences bash against my mind's innermost doors. Had I given biology a run for its money, had I not prized psychological, emotional truth over literal, had it not been as simple as truth, not courage, that propelled me into becoming the man I knew I was, would this woman's ghost be easier to vanquish, as I would more closely resemble it? Could I take her place more easily in Eliza's heart if I'd disguised myself in colour, not revealed myself in short hair and grey suits? I cannot be a rival. Not in my true state. Never before had I wished my untrue state back, and that shame descended on all sides. I had no strength of character if the wishes of someone else made me wish I was someone else, some weaker falser version of myself. 'I don't have to prove anything,' I say to make myself believe it.

'Not to me.' Ash sounds amused, knowing this is no help at all. I am submerged in the feeling that this thing I must have created, this strange drip from my own imagination, is on my side. 'I will always be here,' she said. It wasn't a threat, just a fact she knew would be difficult for me, that we might as well both acknowledge.

'Yes,' I say. 'But you can leave us alone now.' I will always remember what it felt like to put out my hand, and to feel Ash shake it. Ash wasn't competition when I arrived. I did not take Ash as a personal insult. But if all it takes is a simple trick for me to see Ash's face, what's to say there isn't light at both ends of that tunnel. Ash is not my ghost any more than I am Ash's creature.

~

Eliza comes to my room instead of hers, not needing to switch the light on to find the bed. 'Thanks for putting the towels away,' she whispers in the darkness, as she slides in beside me.

'No problem.' No problem at all. I did no such thing. I am almost sure I left them on the bathroom floor after I handed Ash back the hairbrush she forgot, and watched them both disappear, ending the conversation as impossibly as I opened it. 'I think the ghost I raised to haunt me has been laid. So to speak.'

Eliza kisses the side of my face, just below my ear. I turn towards her, the face that was more familiar, more real to me than my own. I had no concern in what she expected to find. She did not expect. She did not assume. She observed, explored. Perhaps the selfishness, the power of the attraction, was the chance to learn to do the same.

If Ash was watching us from the door, it was too dark to see. It was too dark to even see Eliza, the naturalness of her, the identity she'd come to so easily, the body she was so at home in. I understood what it was to be Ashley far more. I understood being yourself by sustained choice, argument and effort, to be comfortable in your own default skin, was a fantasy. Eliza was sure she'd fallen in with the right body, the way when I joined my department I knew I'd fallen in with the right crowd. The house, or Ash – if Ash was there at all – had made itself clear in that from the first, if we accepted its terms. No walls shook, no doorways crumbled, not even inside my own mind. I cannot compete with a ghost, least of all one of my own making. But I will choose to stay. Even when I cannot be sure which of us is haunted. We were here, now; whatever had gone before, we had every right to claim our ever-after and call it happy.

The Other Woman, Part 2

'Please' is the first word I hear her say. Her voice is full of lies, each snotty English sound as beautiful and false as I imagined it. The tears are lies as well: she has no right to them either. 'You don't have to do this.'

'"You don't have to do this,"' I mimic, higher even than my own voice. People always laughed at my voice. But a high voice is the voice of a proper woman, not low and proud like hers, pretending to be what she is not, pretending she belongs in this country when she is the scum my parents would have thrown off our land. 'I thought you were a poet. You should have something better to say.'

No more words at all, she's only crying now. It's been hours since I took the gag off, let her realise no amount of screaming would get through my thick, loyal walls. They know me, these walls. The oxygen of the room tastes big and sweet in my mouth; my tiny, soundproof attic room feels infinite. I am infinite. As infinite now as she ever made me small. Sweat is clogging the mouse-brown rats-tails of her hair, the false power melting from her impossibly young face as I brush out my own, proudly greying hair in the mirror on my dressing table. The frizz of white ends forms a halo around me in the hot orange of the one bare bulb shining down upon us. In the warmth of my light, I see my every frown line and, behind me, the cold fear in her young eyes. Was I really ever that young? She does not understand how lucky she is. She could have taken any man. She should have had a dirty gyppo like herself. She did not have to take him.

'You see?' I indicate my halo in the mirror with the handle of the brush. She cowers in the corner of the old single bed, at the edge of my spotlight. He hadn't lied when he told me she is everything that I am not. But I am everything she should be and I will make her know it. Every tear is a new victory. 'See what God is showing you? A proper woman. A real woman. Not a mistress.'

'Please…' That voice, clear and deep and pure, pretending to be all she is not. She does not belong in this country, in spite of that lying voice. I belong. I have lived here longer than she has been alive. She is vermin. 'Virginie…'

It is strange to hear her say my name; proof that we exist in the same world after all, though hers always seemed so far from mine. I turn and run my dry palm over her soft face, feeling where his kisses went, feeling what he saw with his eyes, his lips. She is everything I've always known is ugly, beneath me, with her long nose and skeleton face. But he saw something else. 'You know we have a son, slut?' I demand. 'You know that you took our son's father?'

'Virginie…' Tears are falling, but something sits deeper than the fear in her eyes. Her toxic sympathy clouds my precious air. How dare she feel sorry for me? I am the powerful one now. There in the mirror is the saint she has wronged. I look into my own eyes for a few seconds, steadying my grip on my hairbrush, on my reality. A mother, a wife. A proper woman. 'You took Paul's father away from him,' I tell our reflections.

'Nick told me you were separated, Virginie.

You'd been in separate bedrooms for years. He said...'

I strike my fingernails across her cheek. My nails are not long, like hers were before I snapped them, not cared for at that smug and sunny corner place on the high street I followed her to every Friday morning, before she'd meet with him in that café that used to be a church – one blasphemy after another – yet mine do the job as well as any. Two trickling lines of blood, a brighter red than her broken talons. She won't be getting those broken nails into anyone else. I look away from her eyes to find my own again. 'You took Paul's father.'

'Paul's twenty-five, Virginie.' Her self-righteous tears are already blurring the edges of the blood I drew. 'He lives in Canada—'

She swallows a gasp as I turn and slap her bloody cheek. My palm comes away buzzing with wet heat, the blood and tears of the enemy. There is something thrilling about being able to touch the ghost that has haunted me, to haunt her back. 'Paul is travelling,' I say. 'Paul is coming back. Children always do.' Nicholas always came back to me. Paul is almost as old now as Nicholas was when made him. Children always come back. The trick is to keep them feeling like children.

'All Nick's friends, all of us knew he lived with the mother of his daughter. That you'd been in separate rooms since Paul was a toddler. It never occurred to me, to any of us—'

'Dirty gyppo!' The hairbrush misses her eye, but I don't follow my throw. I will not think what *all of us, any of us* means, Nicholas's social circle I was not asked to be part of. That is done now. I forgive him. I stay with the mirror, gaze into the certainty of my own eyes, each line, each grey hair, each tear-track reinforcing my pure and righteous anger. 'You do not understand love. I will make you understand. Evil, crazy gyppo.'

'I was born in Chiswick, Virginie. I'm hardly—'

'You are evil! The purest evil!' The gag is still around her neck, her hands. I tighten her neck first. 'I know all about you. With your dark eyes and clever words. You think you are so clever but I know all about you.' I pull the gag back up, silence her again. I don't have to look at how her dark brown hair frames her helpless-pixie face, the silly, girlish look with which she trapped him then wanted to come to his rescue, as if he needed rescuing from me when all the time it was she who was the monster. 'He is safe from you now.'

She's whimpering at last, even if it's only physical pain, gasping against the tears clogging her throat. At last she is the pathetic mess she deserves to be, that I knew was the truth of her; nothing left of herself beyond terror and loss. She is trying so hard to speak under the gag. It sounds like a short sentence, a quiet one. I cannot help being curious. What harm can a question do me now? I pull the gag down, around her neck.

'Tell me how he died,' she says.

'He was mine,' I tell her as my fingers tighten in her hair. And he was. More than my own face, more than anything else I considered my own self was Nicholas, my man. My prize that showed the world who I was. A wife, though we never married. Oh, we nearly did, even went almost as far as the registry office the year after Paul was born. This girl, this hunched and stooping cockroach would not understand how recent that is to me, she is too young to understand how time really feels. But there was always something, some licence not applied for, some paper not signed. But as Paul's mother I was every bit a wife. What truer, deeper bond is there than having a child? Why, if we were not bonded forever, did our fingers tighten round each other's necks the night he told me about this poet, this teacher with whom he thought he'd fallen in love, as if anything that would break up a home could be love? What else was this but a test of my love, the ultimate test, the chance to show him how hard I would fight to keep what was mine?

'I need to know, Virginie.' Her deep voice is still clear through the tears. 'He was on the floor. They found him there, in your kitchen, his hand reaching out for—'

'He knew he had no right to walk away.' I am strong when I look at the mirror; calm and clear. It is only her face that confuses things, her face and its evil gypsy spell.

'You stabbed him slowly.' The tears are falling down her face the way I imagined them. 'When he kissed you goodbye, you were holding a knife...'

'We have a child. A child scarred by his disloyalty.' This pestilence, this cockroach cannot imagine the years of power and love I saw in his eyes, as I demanded he take out his phone and call her, say he wasn't coming after all, that he never would. I knew he'd go, call her again, tell her I made him say those things, that they weren't true, but the only truth that mattered was that I could make him say them. That she and I would know he would never quite be with her, never step through between our past and any other future.

The police are looking for an old woman. They wouldn't recognise me as I arrived back here, the pieces of me in every drawer of this dressing table, purchased in all the right shades to bring me back as I remember myself, my lipstick, my wigs, my eyes scouring the websites until I was perfectly encased in my old self. The woman he loved, the woman he would never have left. Time means nothing; I can buy my past back. They will not be looking for false eyelashes, oxblood lips; will not be looking for who I was before I was old instead. The pieces of me that had fallen away, that I feel drifting back into place with her every tear, her every drop of blood. The pieces of me he was looking for when he found her. I am becoming myself again. I reclaim myself from her. If he saw us both now, he'd love me.

'Please, Virginie, tell me.'

'I could have been a poet like you, a teacher like you. I told you in those letters what you were doing wrong. Those notes left at the café, at the nail bar, where I knew you'd be. I sent you my poetry. To show you what true love, my love, is.' And all she did was send my emails to the police. Just because I called her what she was. A gypsy. A monster. An ugly, deformed cockroach. 'He gave himself to me. Here, on this bed. Did you know that is where I have brought you? His life began with me here. His real life. Before me, with you. That was not his real life. His real life is what I gave him. He owes me everything. This is his womb.' I will show this gypsy, this cockroach. I will show her love and poetry. I will teach her. 'What we created here cannot be uncreated. He is mine.' I grab her cheeks again, breathe her in. 'He wasn't yours. He wasn't leaving again! He would always come back. He will not change, will not grow up. He was nothing before me. He is nothing without me. I am his wife, his mother.'

'You're neither. You never were. Living like that...' She is crying. Our faces are so close to each other I cannot be sure whose tears are which. 'That isn't love.'

'He is mine more truly than you can imagine. He was never going to be yours the way he was mine. He could never let himself. He knew he was always mine.'

'You killed him because he loved me.'

'I had to kill his love.' I dance the knife over her wrist, the long way, the way the videos show you, light enough that there's only a thin white path, no blood yet. But this is the way I will cut, when the time comes. It's the best way. I have studied. She is not the only one who can learn new skills, create the life she imagines. All of it is there, waiting online. You just have to look for it. 'He could not do it without me. His love had to be dead.'

'Virginie. Please.'

I am closer to her now, eye to eye, closer than I could be to my reflection in the dressing table mirror. Does she understand how beautiful she is, how much of a choice was before her? She could have made anyone love her. But I have a job to finish. There needs to be nothing left of their love, and that love will not be gone until she is. I cannot feel free in a world where he chose her over me and she lived. I push he hair from her cheek and turn the knife on its side. 'N for Nicholas,' I say as I carve three little strokes deeper into the place I'd scratched her before, the third to join the two. 'A beautiful letter.' I follow the lines with my finger. 'My north, my south, my north again. Always he returned to me.' As I take my finger away and lick the tip, feel the taste of her in my mouth. 'There are days he returned and we made love, and I imagined I was you, even if he did not.'

'Virginie, please...'

I reach inside my blouse, close to my neck. 'You know what this is?'

She hesitates.

'You cannot fail to recognise it, gyppo.'

Her brow furrows.

'Do not pretend you do not know it. He only ever took it off to shower. Would leave it beside the watch I gave him for his thirtieth birthday, the day I took his virginity and gave him Paul.'

'Thirty?' She is ignoring it. 'That doesn't add up. Paul's only—'

I strike her again. How can she be so cold, so intellectual in full view of her own blood? 'Paul died the first time we made him. We tried again.

He stayed with us the third time. Third and perfect.' I swing the pendant before her eyes. 'Each time Nicholas talked about leaving. I told him he was mine. You say you loved him. Yet you did not miss this. The police did not miss this. And you all claim to love him so much.'

Realisation flickers in her wet, dark eyes. 'Nick's pendant,' she repeats. 'That silver dolphin. I remember...' It is as if she is someone else for a moment, remembering from further away. Why would that be? But then she seems to return to me, to my hands with the dolphin under her eyes, to the knife tracing down from her cheek to her throat. 'Let me touch it?' she asks. 'Let me die holding it.'

I look behind me, even though I know the door is secure, and that the window above us is so high and so small there is nothing to be lost while her feet are attached to the bed. Why should I deny myself what I want most: to witness their final goodbye, to know in my own senses, in my soul, that they will never know each other again?

My knife slices the rope tying her hands. She holds them still, as if in supplication, as if the rope is still there, invisible to me. I drop

Nicholas's dolphin into her palms. She looks down at it, dark eyelashes flickering. I always thought she had to know how beautiful she was. How could he love her and she not know?

All she sees is the dolphin, even as I tighten the cords at her feet. Her eyes have not moved from the pendant in her hands, as if being able to see that is being able to keep him. I put the knife down on the dressing table for a moment, just for a better look, just to take her face in my hands. She looks up from the pendant into my eyes, deeply, as if she's looking for whatever I was looking for when I looked at her, just as deeply though so very far away, from the shadows between the buildings opposite them as they greeted each other outside the café; watching the way their eyes shone like a mirror of each other, as if the pleasure one felt for meeting the other was shining back, reflecting and growing into something I had never seen before in his or any eyes.

I thought if I followed her long enough I would understand what she had, remember what it was to be as young and beautiful as her. But never had that been enough, not on its own. Not to keep him. We needed our dances,

Nicholas and I, towards and away from each other, voices rising and falling, throwing and strangling and yelling and embracing and yelling and strangling and throwing again. He did not show anyone else that passion, what a passionate man I made him. I knew it made Paul stronger, seeing that; showed him before he spoke or understood words that love was something you fought for.

They never did that, Nicholas and this gypsy. All they ever seemed to do was look at each other, and kiss, and smile. I always watched her more than him – her lips, her eyes, like a strange reflection not of body, though perhaps of soul.

Those lips are in front of me now. Those eyes see only me, in my attic room where no one but who I've chosen – only Nicholas – has ever come. Before I know I'm going to, I have placed my oxblood lipstick over that strange gypsy mouth, to feel what he felt, to see how what I was taught was evil and ugly was beautiful and good to the best of men. My tongue, my closed eyes, my wet cheeks probing every possible place anywhere he might have been. I knew that she would not resist. I did not know I would feel her tongue pressing behind her dry lips, kissing me back. Is she kissing me? Or is she imagining I am him? It is both, it is neither, it is something entirely itself and new as I hold her like we held each other, Nicholas and I, in this last and truest place on earth, as I allow all of myself to fall into all of her, all that's left of him that I was denied. I do not want to be myself without him.

She is holding me too tightly. It's just what he would have done. She pushes herself on top of me. Blood roars in my ears. There's a patter of wings on the skylight, a noise as if one of the birds that are my secret world's only audience is bashing against its one high window. But the ceiling is a world away and nothing that far matters.

She presses her hands onto mine, her bound ankles and closed legs pushing her body against mine, strong as a mermaid's tail, as she lies above me.

'Seriously, Holly?' A man's voice. A man's voice from the sky, laughing.

'Nicholas?' My eyes are open, searching.

But what I am seeing makes no sense. There is not much clear beyond Nicholas's gypsy's face, but there is a hand on the gypsy's shoulder. A man's hand, large, protective, a gold band on his wedding finger.

'Are you here, Nicholas?'

'Sorry to disappoint,' the man says. Though he could become a man like Nicholas, really he is a boy, like the gyppo he's barely ten years older than Paul. It is only when he reaches down to secure the free ropes around my wrists that I understand I have let the gypsy out of hers. Even then, the face of the man with his hand on the gypsy's shoulder is still a stranger. A stranger taking my ropes from the gypsy's hands and securing me to my own bed.

And as he works on my wrists, she is sitting up, pushing herself away from my face, working on my ankles, grimacing with pain and amusement as her snapped nails work the ropes. The tears and blood are drying on her cheeks. 'What an entrance, Tom.'

'Had to be, to make it through that window.' He looks at my wrists, satisfied, then returns to stand by the gypsy still working at my ankles. He bends down to kiss her. His wedding ring sparkles as his palm wipes the tears and blood from her cheek, coming away from her face with my lipstick where it had stayed on her mouth. When he moves back, she goes to take something off her tongue. It is a wedding ring, identical to his.

'That's how you look after my stuff?' She spits it into her hand, smiles up at him.

'You're welcome, Holly.'

She gives a coy laugh, nothing like the laugh I watched her and Nicholas exchange outside their cafe. But she is looking at this strange man exactly the way I saw her look at my own man whenever I followed them.

'Why does he call you Holly?' I demand. 'Nicholas called you Joy.'

They both are giggling like children. 'I had no idea her voice was so... sweet,' the man says. He sits on the edge of the bed, pats my halo of greying hair as if I am his dog. 'Funny. I thought you'd be... tall. I always picture really successful bullies being tall.'

'Who is Holly?' My demand is a shriek.

The girl turns towards me. She squats on the floor beside where he sits on the edge of my bed, her broken nails entwined. The pain makes it hard for her to keep her fingers together, but she seems to be enjoying the pain. 'Mirror twins. All the looks, but all the organs the opposite way around. You might say I'm the opposite version of her.'

'But I followed you...'

'Right past her old house. I knew you wouldn't let us see you, but I knew you'd be looking for her. I made sure you saw what you wanted to see. Tom dropped me off around the corner, then he tailed your ridiculous little van. Like I said, Joy and I are opposites. She gave Nick every opportunity she could. Tried to be kind. I'm not kind, Virginie, not like Joy. She's the good one. I'm the efficient one.'

'That, my love, you most certainly are.' The man sits. 'It's a good career, you know, cruelty-free hitperson. We only take contracts where society is served by the removal of a killer, a racist, or in your case both. I still do personal training – I was a dancer – but I'm getting on now. Thirty-two, would you believe? Ancient.' He runs his fingers over his perfect hairline. It makes the silky rustle Nick's did years ago, and a gasp escapes my throat. He continues talking, gazing at the skylight he climbed through. 'Keeps me trim. And anything to help Joy. Joy's not like Holly: has no idea how much better she deserves. Can't say that about you, can we my love?'

'I certainly hope not.' The girl stands beside him, fiddling with his hair. The look on her face is the look her sister gave Nick, each time I followed them. It was the most beautiful thing, watching the man I love look so happy. Their faces so full of love, a love so uncomplicated and blameless I barely recognised it. The soft movement of Holly's fingers in her husband's hair rips through my heart, turns every memory into the sharpest of spikes. 'You wanted to be a teacher, didn't you Virginie?' she says. 'And a poet? Isn't that why Nick told you it's what he'd fallen for? Give you a kick to do something with your life instead of waiting for life to happen to you? I guess we'll never know what you could have done. Maybe you could have been a cruelty-free hitman instead of a murderer.'

'Hitperson,' Tom corrects her, his lips to her ear.

'Hitman,' she corrects him back. 'Like chairman. Actor. Manager. Mankind. One species. A community.' I watch her head turn towards his, the depth of the kiss. She turns to me, a playful curiosity on her lips. 'You know, I was fascinated by you? A woman with a history of racism and physical violence considering my sister the essence of evil? Because of our race, and because Joy fell for a man who claimed he was single? A man you fell for yourself? *That's your idea of evil?* Doesn't that seem *interesting?*'

'Not really,' her husband leans his chin on her shoulder. 'Not interesting. Just really, really wrong.'

'Maybe you're right, Tom. But Joy thought so.' Holly adjusts herself to sits in front of him on the bed, his arms around her waist. 'She was never your enemy, Virginie. You made your own hell, all by yourself. Alone. And that, by the way, is how this story ends.'

'You don't have to do this,' I say, horrified at hearing her words coming from my mouth.

'No,' says the girl. 'That's the beauty of life. We have choices.' She teases the knife over my neck. Her face doesn't change as I feel the movement deepen, becoming a rush, and a lightness, and then it's as if I'm spilling out of myself like water from a glass. Her face, as if beyond a smeared window, still looks so like the one I hate. But that face is fading and fading yet all I see, even when I can't see anything anymore, is my image of her.

Thanks to:
Lucy Coleshill
Colin Dunlop
Neil Mason
Marc Morris

Now available and forthcoming from
Black Shuck Shadows:

blackshuckbooks.co.uk/shadows

Ingram Content Group UK Ltd.
Milton Keynes UK
UKHW020607090323
418167UK00012B/174

9 781913 038991